Book Four

The Archers' |

D1526810

Chapter One

We were standing on the roof of our motelygalley's forward deck castle as we slowly rowed into the Fowey estuary. It was a welcome sight to see the smoke of the cooking fires rising from the little village of Fowey off our port side. Helen was standing with on the roof and so was Harold Lewes, the galley's captain and his sailing sergeant.

I gave a great sigh of relief. Finally, and to my great satisfaction, the rough waters of the channel were behind us. We had made it back to our new home to Cornwall once again. There were great billowing white clouds covering part of the sky and sun, at least for the moment, was shining through a gap between the clouds and was warming us.

"We are almost there, Helen. Restormel Castle, your new home, is a little ways up this river. It is called the River Fowey, by the way, and the little cluster of houses off to the left is Fowey village. The people who live there eat the fish they catch in the sea and the greens and such that they find

in the forest. And sometimes they eat deer and wild boar
and birds that they take in the forest with their bows.

"Funny people, they are; they live here in Cornwall and
always have, but they speak some kind of local gobble no
one can understand. Strange, is it not? Thomas, my brother
who is a priest and knows such things, says they came from
far away just like you, but from a different land somewhere
to the north called Ireland. You will like him, I think; my
brother."

******

We rowed up the Fowey against the current until we
reached our training camp for new archers just below
Restormel Castle. The camp is where the boys and men
who want to go for an archer with our Company have the
required learning put on them. If they are successful with
their arrow pushing and do as they are told, they are
allowed to make their marks on the Company roll and join
us.

Along the way we had rowed around a bend in the river
and come across two boys sitting on the grassy river bank
with crudely fashioned fishing poles. They waved
enthusiastically as we passed and ran a few steps along the
river footpath to keep up with us for a while.

Then the boys saw all of the other galleys coming up the
river behind us. Fishing was ignored. The just stood there

looking back down the river in amazement. Helen and everyone on deck gave them a friendly wave. They quickly recovered from their surprise at seeing so many galleys on the river and waved back.

"Are they biting?" someone shouted over to them.

The boys smiled back at us and then suddenly turned around, listened for a moment, and ran off to the entrance to a narrow dirt path into the heavily wooded forest. Someone's mother must have called.

They were probably from a family of poor squatters or outlaws hiding in the forest since there are no farms along this stretch of the river due to its periodic flooding. There were also no farms on that side of the river because the land had been used for years as a hunting ground for the Restormel lords. That was before we killed the latest of the murdering bastards and took over his holdings to compensate us for the trouble and losses he had caused us and our friends.

Ah well, the boys looked like good lads and we were not much into hunting, were we? *Unless, of course, what we were hunting was a Moorish transport with a fat cargo.* Hunting in the forest was fine and could be good sport, but we found it much easier to raise sheep, cattle, and poultry and kill them whenever we needed something to eat. Besides, we needed more meat to feed the would-be archers we were training and the castle folk than we could ever get by finding deer and boar in the forest to harvest. The boys and their family could stay.

******

Our training camp and old galley our new recruits are initially trained on came into sight as we came around a slight bend in the river. From where we were standing on the castle roof could see it through the trees.

Everything looked very much the same as it had when we left in the spring to sail back to the Holy Land to earn more coins carrying cargos and refugees to safety in our galleys. The same tents and sleeping hovels for the sailors and boat wrights were there along the tree line, and the two dinghies covered with rough cut boards were still moored to the trees along the shore to act as a floating wharf.

Restormel Castle's great stone walls could be seen in the distance beyond the training camp. It looked strong and sturdy even though it was not. But it would be soon.

Helen was wide-eyed and at the sight of the castle and the activity in the camp. She was also, I could tell, more than a little nervous. It was quite understandable since this was all new to her.

She had never been anywhere or done anything until her owner gave her to me. So I did my best to explain.

"Our sailors and apprentice archers, the lads who have come to us because they want to go for an archer with the Company, are kept busy working on the cart paths and the castle's defences when they are not busy in their other duties and being learnt to be archers.

This is the camp where they are filled with learning as to how to push arrows out of longbows and how to use the long-handled bladed pikes that our smiths on Cyprus have begun turning out. Spending all their hours being learnt to be archers and working on our roads and the castle keeps them out of mischief, yes it does. They do it because those who are found full enough of the learning are allowed to make their marks on the Company's roll and join us.

"Over there is one of the two galleys my men and I had left here in Cornwall before we sailed back to Cyprus and the Holy Land was still moored to the same tree that was growing along the riverbank just below our rickety little floating wharf. It is our oldest galley, the one that is so unseaworthy it is never taken beyond the estuary. *And would soon be broken up for firewood as a result.*

The other galley we had left behind had been much more seaworthy. It was nowhere to be seen so it must either be off on an errand or perhaps, God forbid, it had been somehow lost. Perhaps it was off on a short training cruise to show the new recruits how to live and row on one of the Company galleys. I certainly hoped we had not lost it and, truth be told, immediately became slightly worried. Ah well, I would know soon enough.

The two galleys, and also the old cog we had rowed past at the mouth of the river, were used to teach our archers and pike men how to behave and fight in the years ahead when they are aboard a Company galley or fighting an enemy galley or trying to take one of the sailing ships the Moors use to transport cargos in the waters around the Holy Land—the big cargo cogs and ships with their high sides which are so difficult to climb aboard and capture unless you know how.

Teaching our archers and pike men how to board an enemy boat was one of the reasons we had the old cog and a number of sailors were stationed here in addition to the sailors serving on our galleys and transports at Cyprus and elsewhere in the east. We also have a couple of other cogs based here. We use them to move people and supplies among the ports from here to Liverpool and Newcastle, and particularly to and from London.

The other cogs are usually here; I wonder where they are?

Harold himself had moved down to the deck and was standing in our galley's bow ready to throw its mooring line to a couple of ragged-looking men standing on the floating wharf. They looked to be some of our boat wrights by the look of their clothes and the tools they had left on the nearby riverbank when they climbed on the floating wharf to catch the mooring lines.

The two men were a welcome and timely sight, that is for sure; several of our galleys are badly in need of repairs. One of them leaks so severely it is a wonder it made it here without sinking.

Apostos from Cyprus, the sergeant of our boat wrights here in Cornwall, obviously heard the cries of the men who could see and hear us coming. He was walking briskly towards the little wharf as we were mooring, and he was doing so with a big welcoming smile on his face and his hand held up in a friendly greeting. And there is Jeffrey, the sergeant in charge of the archers' training, by God.

I wonder why Jeffrey is here. Normally he is at Restormel where we train the apprentice archers and barrack them.

Apostos and Jeffrey both got big handshakes and enthusiastic claps on their shoulders from me and then from Harold as we climbed over our galley's deck railing and on to the unsteady little wharf. It was good to see them again; it surely was. Helen hung back.

"Hello, Jeffrey, it is good to see you. What brings you down here with the people who have to work for their bread? Going for a sailor, are you?"

"My God no, William. No sea pox for me. But it is good to see you, Captain, and that ugly old sailor with you as well. Have a good trip, did you and the lads?"

Yes, we have so many Williams among our archers we have all ended up being scribed on the company roll with a second name. William Tamar, William Farmer, William Smith, and so on and so forth. I am the William who captains the company so now I am sometimes Captain William of William Captain or just William.

"Yes we did, Jeffrey, yes we did. We hit Almeria and got away with almost nothing; but then we hit Cadiz and made off with fourteen Moorish galleys and a very nice cog. We sent them off to Cyprus with prize crews, did not we? I will tell you all about it when we have a chance to hoist a bowl together."

Jeffrey and Harold and I talked about many things as we stood and watched as the rest of our ten galleys came in one after another and tied up to trees along the riverbank. But most of our talk was about how soon we can get as many as possible of our galleys resupplied and headed back to Cyprus and the need to have our two leakers pulled ashore to be repaired and how long it might take.

And, of course, the most important question of all, at least so far as I am concerned—how many fully trained archers do we have available to immediately send back to Cyprus with their own longbows?

Yes, I know; I will soon be having the same conversation with Thomas, but we have not a day to spare and I want Jeffrey and everyone else to get started. There is no time to lose; we have an obligation to the merchants who have begun acting as our agents in the Holy Land ports to quickly replace the galleys we sent to Constantinople and Antioch.

We now have enough galleys, of course, because of all those we took out of Cadiz a couple of weeks ago, and we can always find sailors and pilots in the ports along the way; what we are mostly missing are archers with longbows and bladed pikes who know how to fight on both land and sea— the ones we have taken to sometimes calling our Marines.

******

I did not have to wait long to see my son and my priestly brother. There was a great "hello" and here they came hurrying down the cart path from the castle. Someone standing on the castle wall must have seen the galleys coming up the river and they have come to greet us.

And it was a right merry time when they reached us— George broke into a run and was totally out of breath when he jumped right into my arms. So I held him up off the ground and danced him around and around with many hugs and kisses whilst I was trying to shake the hand of my priestly brother Thomas and hug him too. What I still remember most was being absolutely delighted because George was so pleased to see me. It was a happy time— everywhere men were beaming at each other and shaking hands and everyone was talking to everyone else at the same time.

"It is good to see you, young man; I have missed you, I truly have. And you too, Thomas. You are both a good sight for these tired eyes. And by God, George, I think you have grown bigger. Good on you, my boy, good on you."

I began to get things underway after things settle down a bit. Apostos, Harold, and Jeffrey listened intently and I kept my arm around George whilst I explained to Thomas and my sergeants what needed to be done and why. Helen remained quietly behind me on the galley's deck.

"Thomas, I will explain later, but we need to get as many of these galleys as possible resupplied and turned around and started back to Cyprus as soon as they can be made ready. And they must go out with as many archers and men-at-arms as you can safely spare. Harold will be in command as the fleet's master sergeant; I will be staying in Cornwall a while longer, at least until next spring and maybe even longer."

I continued after a pause whilst I motioned Helen to come down from the galley where she had been quietly waiting to join us.

"Oh, and Apostos, a couple of these galleys need significant repairs; the ones right behind us. And one of them probably should be pulled ashore immediately before it sinks—the one over there where the men are still bailing hard. But once you get it ashore, I want you to ignore it. Concentrate your men on repairing those that need minor repairs so Harold can lead them back to Cyprus as soon as possible."

Helen's walking up behind me caused a bit of a stir. Most of the sergeant captains who sailed here with me had seen her but Thomas and George did not know about her at all.

"Uh, George, Thomas, everyone, this is Helen. She is my . . . uh . . . uh. . . . She is with me." *I could not bring myself to say my slave or my gift.* Fortunately Thomas understood immediately. He promptly gave her a big smile and a welcoming hug. She beamed a great and somewhat thankful smile at him, and then a shy one at George.

******

All afternoon our horse carts, some pulled by horses and others by men mustered for the purpose, moved back and forth between the boat camp and Restormel—carrying coin chests and various of Helen's purchases and other things up to the castle; returning with amphora jars full of oil and sacks of corn to feed the men on the galleys.

Thomas moved quickly, and after a short delay, cattle and sheep began being driven in to the boat camp to be slaughtered so the newly arrived men could eat their fill and regain their strength. Geese and ducks and chickens and firewood arrived as well, and fires sprang up everywhere to burn the meat and cook flat breads.

It had been a long voyage without proper meat, and the men did well at Almeria and Cadiz; they earned it all. Later in the afternoon, the archers marched up to the castle and enjoyed a second feast. They would stay at Restormel until the galleys were ready to return to Cyprus; the sailors would stay here at the camp and continue to live on their galleys.

Later, after the sun finished passing overhead, there was a real dinner in Restormel's great hall—for George and the boys, Helen, all the senior sergeants, and a couple of Augustinian priests who said they were passing through on their way to hold services at Launceston Priory or join it, I was not sure which. Either was fine so long as they did not try to put down roots as parish priests.

The priests probably stopped here for a last good meal before walking on to the priory. Tonight it was ducks and geese, ox joints, and suet pudding.

The talk was merry and the boys were in awe of Helen and spent most of the evening playing "throw fingers" games with her; the newly arrived sergeants captaining the galleys were mostly just in awe—they had never been in a great hall before let alone supped in one as members of its lord's entourage.

And I am a lord, even though I am landless and poor. I still find it hard to believe and a lot of people still are not sure. I may have been born a serf, but I bought my title fair and square with the coins we took off the thieving bishop who tried to murder us—so here I am, by the grace of God

and a couple of bloody knives. I would not have done it if
Thomas had not said it would be useful in the days ahead.

Thomas and I finally had an opportunity to share some ale and talk without anyone else around to listen. That was later in the evening when the sergeants had downed a parting bowl and gone off to their beds. We waited until George and the boys were in bed and a place had been found for Helen and me.

Once we were alone, I brought Thomas up to date about Constantinople and our affairs in the east and explained why we needed to send all our available galleys and men to Cyprus as soon as possible. He laughed uproariously when I told him how Helen arrived as a gift from the merchants—and a very fine one indeed, he agreed.

Then Thomas got serious and leaned forward over his bowl of ale.

"Trouble is brewing, little brother, big trouble. One of the Germans who claims to be the Holy Roman emperor is holding King Richard for ransom, a big ransom. We have received parchments from the Church and from Longchamp ordering us to help pay it. We have also received parchments from both Prince John and his man in London ordering us not to provide a single coin."

"We do not owe anything to Richard or to the Church or Longchamp," was my irate response. "Do not give them a single copper coin, not one."

"Of course not, I am not that daft, am I? I told them we had already spent all our coins by either giving them to the Pope for his prayers or using them to pay sailors and fighting men to rescue Christians fleeing the Saracens—and reminded them Cornwall is so poor that even the Romans did not build a road to it."

Thomas smiled as he thought about how to tell me what he had done. He was obviously proud of himself and was going to enjoy the telling of his tale. Then he laughed out loud and continued.

"What I did, my dear little brother, was send a parchment to each of them reminding them Cornwall is mostly a home for fishermen and,except for the tin mines whose revenues all go to the Crown, it produces no revenues because its lands are so poor and sparsely populated. It has, I pointed out to each of them, only a handful of monasteries and a few poor churches whose lands are so poor they cannot support a priest.

"To placate John, I added in your name a commitment not to send a single coin for Richard's ransom; to placate Richard, I told Longchamp and the nuncio you had recently impoverished yourself by sending all the coins you would taken from the heathen pirates directly to the Pope at the request of his papal nuncio in Cyprus. I also told them you had pressed Cornwall's tin miners to produce more tin and tin revenues for the realm."

"Did we really do some of that?" I asked Thomas a bit incredulously.

"Well, not really; but it sounded good, do not you think? Actually, I did tell the overseers of the tin mines to increase their output at the same time I told them they had to free their slaves. But of course, I did not send any coins to the Pope or anyone else in your name. I am not daft, am I? The Pope would probably never see them and, if he did, he would almost certainly just piss them away on his entertainments and women."

Thomas continued after a pause for a sip of ale.

"I do not think we have anything to worry about. Longchamp and the Pope's man would not know you did not send your coins to the Pope and they will not be able to ask him or the Cyprus nuncio, will they?" *Or will they? It is a pity we are not the ones carrying parchments and people between London and the east.*

"William, we would know who was saying what and to whom if our galleys and cogs were the ones carrying the parchments and messengers between London and Rome. Maybe we should be posting some of our galleys and cogs in London and Rome instead of stationing most of them in the Holy Land or here. What do you think?"

******

The sun shining in my eyes and the calls of the roosters woke me up the next morning. Restormel was a huge castle with a splendid stone keep consisting of three perfectly round rooms stacked on top of each other and a fine stone staircase connecting the top two rooms to the great hall below them. And, of course, we have a cellar extending under the great hall and part of the bailey. That is where our food supplies are stored, and there are cells for the keeping of people we consider to be felons and such.

The top floor is where the coin and treasure chests are stored and where we keep extra bales of arrows and other weapons in case of a siege. Thomas and the boys sleep on string beds on the second floor. Helen and I pushed aside some of the coin chests and had our string bed and such carried up to the coin room from Harold's galley.

It was quite comfy. We had our own string bed in a cheery corner and a piss pot all to ourselves with two archers' slits to let in the sun. There are even wooden plugs we can put into the slits to keep out the cold and dangerous night air. But best of all, at least according to Helen, an old leather galley sail has been hung to divide the room and give us some privacy if someone comes for coins or weapons.

Helen is quite peculiar about our privacy and accommodations; yes, she is. Even before we went to sleep last night she asked if a shite pot was available and put some of the carpets she fetched from Constantinople on the floor stones to hide their cold from our feet.

Helen gave the sweetest little snore as I rolled off the bed, rubbed my eyes, scratched my bollocks to bother the lice, and thought about putting on my chain mail. I think not; here I am safe even if I do not wear it. So I gathered up my clothes from where I threw them last night when Helen got playful, hoisted my bollocks and dingle into my codpiece, slipped on my leather shoes and pants, and put my tunic back on without my chain mail under it.

Whilst I was getting dressed, I could hear the boys whispering and giggling in the room below and could not keep myself from smiling. It is a wonderful morning and I am so glad to be back with all the comforts and pleasures of home.

Helen's still asleep, so I think I will piss and shite outside this morning so as not to wake her. And who would have ever thought I would be the lord of such a fine place without even having to buy the Pope's prayers and such to get it—all Thomas and I had to do was kill the thieving bishop who tried to murder us and start using his coins. Then one thing led to another and here we are.

So down the stairs and out the door I went, and then I walked through the bailey and climbed the three steps up to the stone chute in the curtain wall. That is where Thomas insists everyone inside the walls piss and shite. It is a useless bother, of course, but it makes him happy. It is probably why the moat is so slimy and the fish taste so bad.

Harold was just coming down the stairs from the shite hole as I was climbing up.

"How do things look?" I asked as I continued on up to take a desperately needed piss. I looked over my shoulder at him whilst he answered. *Some things wait for no man.*

"Well, we have already got more than enough supplies and livestock off the manors to feed ourselves on the way back to Cyprus. The problem is we have only five usable galleys and maybe a couple more if we have a week or two to caulk them. But that is about it. William Forester's galley came in with a badly cracked rib just off the keel. He was lucky it did not give way and sink out from under him."

"What about the training galley or those off to London? What shape are they in? Can you take them and leave some of the three being repaired for training and recruiting?"

Later in the morning, Harold and Thomas and I talked about many such important matters as we walked down the muddy cart path to the boat camp. What I heard was very encouraging.

We had many more new archers in camp than I had expected—almost two hundred and fifty who were thought to be good enough with longbows to be sent out to Cyprus for Yoram and Henry to use. Even if we took them all, it would leave well over a hundred partially trained apprentices here to guard the place whilst their arms are getting stronger and they finish their training.

"My God, Thomas, no wonder Restormel seems to be crawling with archers. It is. We must have over seven hundred of them here if the veterans who just came in on our galleys are included."

Harold reminded me of even more.

"Do not forget there are also a couple of archers from among the slaves we freed from the Cadiz galleys and thirty or forty more who will probably sign up to train as apprentice archers, if the past is any guide; maybe more if we push them."

Freed galley slaves make good archers if they are still healthy. They have got strong arms from all the rowing, do not they?

It seems word has gotten out about our company being a good company for archers and would-be archers to join. According to what Thomas told me last night, we are getting more and more men who show up wanting to join us as apprentice archers. Some are walking for days to get here.

And more may be on the way. As I was told last night whilst we were supping, the weather was good a few days ago so one of the cogs, the little one with the short mast, went off to London to pick up any men and boys our recruiting parties might have sent to the ports along the way. According to Thomas, it should be back any day now.

"Well," I told Harold, "plan on all the seaworthy galleys leaving as soon as possible. We are not going to wait for the galleys needing repairs. They can come out on their own later."

It is usually safe for war galleys to travel alone, particularly ours. The pirates are looking for undefended cargo transports with valuable cargos and sailors to seize, not galleys full of archers to fight for no gain in the unlikely event they win.

* * * * * *

Later that warm, sunny morning, I was walking back from the boat camp when I got to thinking about all the troubles and fighting we had last year and the troubles I had heard about here in England. For some reason, I suddenly became very uneasy, almost worried, about the future and my plan to send our archers back to Cyprus. I began to think Thomas and I should somehow change our plans—perhaps send some and maybe even all of our new apprentice archers out to Henry on Cyprus for their training and keep more of the experienced archers here for our protection, maybe all of them.

By the time I crossed the drawbridge and headed for the cook shed, a misting drizzle had started and I had reached a decision as to what to do—I was going to keep almost all the archers and archer apprentices here over the winter and intensify their training.

And my head is so addled with thinking that I do not watch where I am stepping and almost take a fall; the stones in the courtyard are certainly slick.

And that is what I told Thomas.

"Thomas, I have been doing some thinking and I think we need to change our plans. I am concerned about the murderous lady, or whatever she is, Alicia, Baldwin's wife.

"Think about it. She is a countess living a good life right here in Restormel Castle with Baldwin—and she gets him to attack her widowed sister and nieces in Bossiney Castle so he can evict them and add Bossiney to their holdings."

"Then, after we killed Baldwin and took Restormel, she betrothed herself to Baldwin's cousin, FitzCount of Launceston—and she went right back to once again try to eliminate her sister and her little nieces. And this time she was able to get them killed before we could finish off FitzCount and add his keep at Launceston to our holdings."

Thomas nodded his head in agreement and motioned for me to continue. *I am pretty sure Thomas knows where I am going with this but he wants to hear me say it.*

"Alicia is totally mad, eh? So what worries me is not knowing what she is going to do next. Will she be satisfied now that her sister and nieces are dead? I hope so, but it is starting to worry me because we do not know where she is or what she is doing.

"So I have made up my mind—I am going to send our new and totally untrained men out to Cyprus and keep all of our archers and apprentice archers and all the men Henry trained to use the new bladed pikes here with us in Cornwall.

"We can replace the archers on the Cyprus-bound galleys with the new recruits. Henry can learn them to be archers in Cyprus; and the archers who had not been through Henry's pike training can be learnt how to walk together and use the new pikes here instead of from Henry on Cyprus.

"We brought almost all of our new bladed pikes to England from Cyprus because we do not need them on the galleys and it is not likely we will need them in the Holy Land. If we have to fight out there, it is likely we will be fighting on our ships or behind our walls rather than facing charging knights. It is here in Cornwall, marching to fight an invader is where we are likely to be caught out in the open and need them."

"I agree with you, William, I really do. You are right that we need to stay strong here in Cornwall—what with that devil woman probably wanting Restormel and

Launceston back, and all the kings and would-be kings arguing and fighting about who should pay for their ransoms and wars."

"I am glad to hear you agree, Thomas, I really am. Besides, the archers would not be needed on our galleys if all we are going to do is carry refugees—no one wants to chance a fight with one of our galleys. They know it is not likely to be carrying anything of value and might well have some of our archers and their longbows on board to take them instead of the other way around."

Then Thomas smiled and added something to which I could only smile back and nod my head to show my agreement.

"And, most of all, I am glad you are going to keep the archers here because keeping George safe and learning him and the boys to scribe and sum is much more important than earning a few more coins in the Holy Land. It is the only way our plan can succeed. We have already got enough coins in our chests to last us quite some time, many years actually."

******

Later in the afternoon, Thomas and I stood on the bank of the river and waved farewell as the first of our galleys rowed down the river heading for Cyprus with a crew of sailors and seven dozen or so of our new recruits and former slaves doing the rowing—and then watched in amazement a few hours later when it came right back up the river towing one of our cogs coming in from London with almost a hundred new recruits, and an important rumour.

Towing the cog and its news and archer recruits up the river to us before heading across the channel to France and on to Cyprus was a right good decision by the cog's sergeant captain, Alexander, the archer sergeant from Hassocks who used to be a smith's apprentice. That is for sure; so I went on board and told him so in front of his men. He was very pleased.

Chapter Two

A question of danger.

"Richard has been ransomed and he might be coming to England! Can the rumour be true? Will there be an actual war between him and John, do you think?"

That was what I asked Thomas as I kept waving my hand in a useless effort to drive away the swarm of biting bugs buzzing around my face. The day was warm and the sun was finishing its pass overhead as we walked up the cart path back to Restormel to eat in the great hall. The path was still muddy from this morning's rain and heavily rutted from all the supply wagons moving along it.

I wonder why the bugs are only around the river and come out so much just as the sun finishes passing overhead and goes down over the horizon?

"Of course, it could be true. They have been raising money for his ransom all year and of course he will come to England if it is paid—he is the King. And it is been a long time since he has last been here. Besides, he needs to settle things with John."

"I know that, of course, I do. And it worries me," I said with a rather ill-humoured tone to my voice as I kicked a rock off the path. Then I asked the question that was really bothering me.

"But what will it mean for John and for us if Richard comes to England? Do you think they will fight; they are brothers, after all?"

What I am really asking Thomas is what he thinks will happen to the lands and keeps we took and the earldom we bought with so many of our coins.

"God only knows. But it probably would not be good."

******

Days turn into weeks as our veterans drilled the new men on walking together and using their longbows and the new, long-handled pikes with blades and hooks we were making on Cyprus. It was a grand summer made better by Helen's happiness at discovering I had no wife.

Then word came in from the sailor sergeant of one of our cogs which comes in from London with a load of wheat and salt for our siege reserves—he saw a ship with Richard's flag at the next wharf whilst he was boarding some new recruits and taking on the amphoras of salt and the sacks of the corn we have been buying to build up our siege reserves.

We know how important reserves of food and arrows are during a siege, do not we ever. Firewood to cook the bread is important too, of course.

******

Within days, other reports came in verifying the sergeant captain's story. There is no longer any doubt about it, Richard is back on England's throne and he was trying to raise money for yet another one of his wars—this time in France.

It seems during the years Richard was off crusading, several of the great lords of the French king, the crazy Capet on the throne in Paris, began taking over some of Richard's vast estates along the border between France and Normandy. Richard wants them back even if it means yet another war—which it almost certainly will.

"I have an idea," Thomas said, and then he explained it to me.

"You know, brother, it might just work."

"Worth a try, eh?"

Two days later, one of the galleys being prepared for Cyprus suddenly had its destination changed and more rowers and archers were temporarily added to its crew.

****** *Thomas*

William and the boys walked down the muddy cart path with me to see me off and wish me well. It was a murky day with drizzling rain, and I was off for London with almost a dozen of our best men as guards, a chest with a goodly amount of coins in it, and a couple of hastily drafted parchments carefully rolled up and stashed in one of the leather cylinders used these days by messengers. *I am sure you have seen them; the ones with the carrying strap so the messenger can sling it over his shoulder and walk or ride with his hands free.*

What I hope to do is visit the papal nuncio and William Longchamp at Richard's court, *and preferably the nuncio first*. If I find either or both of them, I will try to do what is inevitably necessary when dealing with such important representatives of the Church and the King— bribe them to sign the orders and proclamations I have drafted for their masters to sign.

The channel was stormy and we had a difficult trip what with having to constantly row against unfavourable winds. But we were well crewed with strong rowers, and four days later, when the sun would be straight overhead if we could see it through the overcast sky, we finally reached the mouth of the Thames and began threading our way through the fog and the crowded shipping.

London is always a busy port and today was no exception. It took hours of rowing around the edge of the great harbour before Simon, our galley's sergeant captain, finally saw some unused wharf space.

We had barely banged into the stone quay when a churlish little fellow wearing a funny hat looked down at us from the quay, informed us he was the quay master, and told us to fuck off and go away; the space was taken.

The quay master was a bit hard to understand because he talked in the sing-song voice and dialect of a long-time Londoner. But he backed off quickly when Simon responded by telling him we were willing to pay a few coins for the right to tie up for a few days, but if we have to leave immediately the only thing certain about our leaving is that he will be coming with us—chained to a rowing bench and helping us to row to Cyprus.

Our quay must usually be used by cogs because I had to stand on the galley's deck railing with Simon and one of his men steadying me to climb up on to the quay. It took some doing, but I was finally able to reach the quay carrying my mitre and crosier and so did the men who were coming with me as my guards and helpers. We were finally ashore in London—me and ten men. Peter Sergeant was with me as my second.

According to William, Peter was initially assigned to Antioch but at the last minute one of the two English archers we signed up in Latika, John, the son of John from Liverpool, took his place. The other archer from Latika, poor soul, died at Cadiz when Phillip's galley was taken. At least, for his sake, I hope he died instead of being captured.

The very first thing I did after I climbed up on the quay was walk to the door of a nearby chandlery and begin inquiring as to the whereabouts of Richard and his court. The portly chandler and his clerks did not have a clue and neither did any of the cart drivers, chandlers, and passers-by I asked.

I was left to guess where Richard might be and my best guesses were Beaumont Palace where he was born or his stronghold at Windsor Castle. *What is really strange is that most of the people I talk to do not even know who the King is, let alone where he and his court might be located.*

Similar inquiries were made during our brief visits to inform the men in the customs house they will not be collecting any taxes or fees from us because we are not bringing in any cargo from abroad. I also talked to a fellow priest I found standing at the door of a nearby church. Everyone seemed to know that the King had returned—but no one was sure where he might be. All they each had heard were rumours in their locals, the taverns and whorehouses they frequented.

The most common rumour had the King at Windsor. Well, if the King's at Windsor then that is where his court and courtiers such as Longchamp and the nuncio will almost certainly be. On the other hand, it is a long way to Windsor and I do not want to travel all the way there just to find out I have pissed away my time and coins on a wild duck chase.

There was nothing to do but go to the one person who was almost sure to know the whereabouts of Richard and his court—the devious and lying keeper of Prince John's wardrobe, Wilfrid Blunt.

I know where Blunt lives. It is where I bribed him last year to buy William's earldom from Prince John after we killed the old Earl and took the treacherous bastard's castle at Restormel. The problem, of course, is a visit to Blunt might be dangerous. There is no telling what John or Blunt will think or do if they find out I am looking for Longchamp or know we have taken so much of Cornwall.

It seems I have no choice. But at least I know where Blunt is likely to be. I thought about hiring a sedan chair and have my guards walk behind it whilst I was carried through London's foul streets. But I decided against it when I saw a stable on a lane near the quay.

None of my guards know how to ride horses and I am not very good at it myself, so I left an outrageously large deposit of two gold bezant coins and hired two horse carts and two hostlers from the stable—and off we clattered to visit John's wardrobe with my guards sitting in the carts and me up next to the hostler on the driver's bench. Peter was sitting next to the hostler on the other wagon.

I have got to talk to William again about some of our men being learnt to ride horses; and, of course, to do that we will have to buy more horses—the dozen or so we have now are already overly busy carrying messages and pulling ploughs and carts.

******

The horse carts carrying my ten guards and me clattered and sloshed their way through the foul and smoke-filled streets to Prince John's walled compound next to the river. I could see my guards staring at the city and talking and gesturing as we bounced along. Most of them have never been to London before. They are obviously amazed at its size and smell and how closely packed together everyone lives. *As I am every time I visit. It is incredibly large; there must be almost fifty thousand people living here.*

It had not rained to clear the air since yesterday, so we could not see very far ahead through the foggy smoke that hung over the city and black soot was covering everything including the piles of fresh shite that the rain had not yet dissolved and washed away. It was a good thing the hostlers know where we wanted to go. It would be easy to get lost in such a big city.

I would hate to be walking out of here after it turned dark. I would probably slip on the street slime and get robbed or worse whilst I was trying to get back on my feet.

When we reached the gate of John's great stone house, it was instantly obvious that Richard was back—the crowd of petitioners and toadies in front of John's gate and inside his bailey was much smaller than it was when I was here last year.

My shout brought an attendant over to the gate—who tersely told me the price of entering to see Blunt, morosely accepted my coins, and gestured for me to enter through the gate and into the courtyard. *At least this time it did not take as many coins to get past the gate guard and in to see Blunt.*

A young dandy standing inside the gate arrogantly beckoned me to follow him and headed off without even waiting to see if I was following. We entered the building through a very heavy wooden door and he led me down a corridor to an empty room—and held out his hand for more coins as he sneered and ordered me to "wait here."

It was all I could do to smile and give him a few coppers from my purse; I had to fight the urge to spit in his hand or stick it with the knife strapped to my wrist. His disdain and arrogance so bothered me I had to piss—so I pissed on the wall after he walked out. And I obviously was not the only one who had recently done so; Blunt must be having a busy day.

Blunt's greeting was effusive and friendly when he finally showed up. He did not seem at all embarrassed because he gulled me into paying so much for William's earldom last year without mentioning that he knew Longchamp was similarly selling the title to FitzCount at the same time. I am not even sure he knows we killed FitzCount to avenge Lord Edmund's family and protect William's title.

I told Blunt the truth, well, part of it at least—that I was looking for the papal nuncio because we want the Pope to charter a new military order whose priests who will only serve when they are on ships and, of course, collect tithes and donations from the passengers they carry in exchange for the Pope's prayers for their safety. The Earl of Cornwall would be its hereditary commander. *It is part of our plan for George and my schoolboys when they grow up and join us.*

"It would be a new source of revenue for His Holiness," I explained. "And more people might become pilgrims and take the risk of sea voyages if they know they will be travelling with the Pope's priests and his prayers."

I could see Blunt's mind feverishly working; it is a church matter so he knows a lot of coins are going to change hands along the way before anything gets resolved. He was trying to think of some way he can insert himself into the process and get some of them.

"That is an imaginative idea and it will be expensive, of course," Blunt finally answered. "Perhaps Prince John and I can assist in some way."

"Yes, I am sure you both could be of great assistance if the Pope's nuncio approves of the idea—that is why I am here. I want to enlist your assistance and support for the idea and, of course, help cover whatever your expenses might be. Doing such a thing is bound to be complex and there will be a lot of expenses to be covered." *Including some for you.*

"In any event, I have been ordered to speak directly to the nuncio and ask him to submit the necessary parchments to the Pope. Do you know where I might find the nuncio?"

Did you notice, as Blunt surely did, that I was telling him I had been ordered to speak directly to the nuncio; not asked, ordered, so no intermediary such as himself can do it for me?

I asked my question as I put a small purse on the table and watched Blunt's eyes light up as he reached for it.

I am not just buying Blunt's help with the nuncio; I am keeping him sweet for the future. John might win, mightn't he? I doubt it myself but one never knows, does one?

"He is at Windsor, last I heard. Prince John is there too. Richard and Prince John seem to have reconciled, or so John hopes in order to keep his head. I am staying here to hold his castle for him, so to speak, whilst he is there paying homage to his elder brother, the King. None of Richard's women have birthed a son so it appears John will be his heir until they do.

"There will be peace between them if John is proclaimed as his successor, and it would be a very good thing for everyone if he is. Wars are expensive, you know."

"They are? Oh, how interesting. I did not know any of that, of course. Cornwall being so poor and distant we never get any news. Just tin mines and poor fishermen, you know. The realm owns the tin so there are no revenues for the Earl; that is why Earl William has to look to the sea and ships. But he and his people do their best with what little God has granted to their lands."

Might as well put a plug in for low taxes whilst I have a chance, particularly if John is to be the heir.

"It is no secret, not even from Richard; Lord William supports John and intends to keep doing so even though his purse is so slim. Prefers him to Richard, does not he? Probably something to do with Richard's behaviour on his crusade."

Like killing the people who surrender to him because he promises to free them and then running away and abandoning his men.

******

It was getting to evening as we reached the outskirts of London. In any event, I took a bug-filled room at an inn outside the city wall for us to sleep in, my men and I that is—the hostlers will sleep in their carts so the stable's carts and horses do not get stolen.

We left early the next morning to travel the old Roman road from the city walls to Windsor. The road was full of ruts and busy with traffic coming and going in both directions, and every hour or so we reached a small village or a manor.

The sun had come out and the wind was blowing towards the city, so there was no fog and smoke out here in the countryside. It is hard to explain but everyone's spirits, both ours and the people travelling the road, seemed to be lifted by the good weather.

Peter and my guards travelled with their bows and swords close at hand, and rightly so because of the outlaw bands which are known to be infesting the roads. It was a generally peaceful scene, however, and their swords were sheathed and their bows unstrung. I was wearing my bishop's gown and mitre so I smiled and waved my cross cheerfully about as travellers approached us from the front or we passed them because they were moving slowly. *Makes everyone feel better, does not it?*

Many of the people on the road appeared to be serfs and slaves walking or pulling carts piled high with grass they were bringing in to feed their lords' livestock over the coming winter. They pulled off the road for us as they must and, somewhat similarly, every hour or so we ourselves had to pull over or slow down for gentry in a cart or carriage. I waved my cross at them too.

I am tired. I did not sleep a wink because I made a mistake and gave the landlord a coin to hire a woman for the men to share. The resulting talking and all the noise they made kept me up most of the night. I should have told them to use her in the street.

******

Windsor Castle looked impressive when we first saw it in the distance, and it was almost certain the King is here with his court. At least, it seemed likely because I could see his great flag on the castle keep.

Richard may be here, but I am still not sure if the Pope's nuncio is here with him. So before we drove on up to the castle gate, I decided to stop at Saint Peters, the local parish church of Windsor Village to inquire and, perhaps, take a place for the night for my men and I.

I am not planning on going anywhere near the King if the nuncio is not here. I am wary because I am not sure if Richard knows I am William's brother or if he knows we supported John and did not help ransom him—and I surely do not want to find out if he is upset about it. He is a killer, you know—even when he gives his word, he cannot be trusted to keep it unless you are a fellow king and sometimes not even then.

Saint Peter Church's priest was at home in his parsonage next to the church. He greeted me suspiciously when I knocked on the door to call upon him. Father George was once again obviously not at all impressed by me being a bishop but he did kiss my ring and tell me he thinks the nuncio is in the castle with the court. He had seen him riding in the King's entourage when it came past the church three or four days ago.

The priest's arrogance and Saint Peter's being such a fine parish with a good parsonage means the priest is probably someone who is considered special. He was undoubtedly either a royal bastard or the younger son of some noble family. Or it could be he is wary because he thinks I am going to try to cadge a meal or a place to sleep off him—and probably it is both since he undoubtedly gets a lot of requests for food and shelter from bishops and priests when they visit the castle.

But the priest's eyes certainly lit up and he quickly reached for the coin I offered if he and his comely young housekeeper would feed me and my men and let us sleep on the church's dirt floor tonight. Then it was off to the castle gate I went with four of my guards in one of the horse carts.

The Pope may order us priests to be celibate, but the Pope's not the only hypocrite in the Church if the housekeeper's baby bump means anything. And who am I to throw stones, eh?

Getting into the castle to see the nuncio takes some doing even though I am wearing the robes and mitre of a bishop and have an entourage of guards. An officious sergeant with the King's coat of arms embroidered on his tunic eyes me sceptically and demanded to know who I am and what I want.

"I am the Bishop of Cornwall and I am here to see the papal nuncio."

"Do you have an appointment?"

"Of course not, I just arrived in London yesterday. Just tell the good man I am here and let him decide for himself. God will bless you—and so will I—if you hurry."

My offer of a blessing to the sergeant and a bit of the necessary—a few coins to sweeten him—soon had one of his men scurrying off to announce me. I took the opportunity to walk a few steps away from the gate and relieve myself of the bad fish I had eaten last night at the inn. *My God that smells; salted cod I think it was.*

******

Almost an hour passed and I was sitting with my back against the castle's stone wall dozing, upwind of last night's fish, when the papal nuncio walked up to me. I jumped up to kiss his ring and his welcome was effusive and brotherly— as well it should be given the size of the purse he had received last year when the Archdiocese of Devon and Cornwall was unexpectedly split and I accepted the awesome responsibilities of heading up the newly re-established diocese of Cornwall even though it was so poor and had so few priests to find coins for me.

"My, this is ambitious and unique," was the nuncio's only comment as he nodded his head after he read the parchment through and then read it again. "It will certainly be very difficult to convince the Holy Father to agree to all this."

He was telling me that he can convince the Pope, but that it will cost me a lot of coins to get the Pope to sign it.

"Of course it will be difficult, Eminence, but there is no doubt God desires such a special order of priests, and the Church will greatly benefit from the tithes of the Christians the new military order of poor landless sailors protects. So it is something that must be done; and, of course, there will be great expenses associated with its establishment which will have to be covered by Lord William and his men." *What will it cost me?*

The good man agreed—and then added something most distressing.

"It will be quite expensive, of course. But will you be able to pay now that King Richard has just recognised a claim to the earldom of Cornwall and its lands put forth by Sir Harold Cornell of Derbyshire, the man who claims to be the cousin and heir of the late Lord Baldwin of Restormel Castle." *Say, what?*

"What was that you just said?"

＊＊＊＊＊＊

The nuncio listened intently as I tried to explain the significance for the King and the Pope's treasury if William and his men are forced to leave Restormel Castle and William decided to return to Cyprus. *I feel terrible—perhaps if I had gotten here a couple of days ago this might not have happened.*

For the King, it would almost certainly mean the end of William's payments to the Crown which are larger than the Derby knight can possibly pay. Why will the new Earl pay fewer coins to the King? Because Cornwall's revenues are so small for its Earl, whereas William as the captain of a successful company of archers can sometimes supplement the taxes he pays to the King with the coins he earns in the Holy Land carrying refugees and pilgrims.

But the King's revenues being reduced is not all, I explained to the rapt nuncio—who obviously saw the size and availability of the purses he might receive from William "to send to the Pope" sailing away to Cyprus before his very eyes.

It is all ox shite about the Pope getting more coins from us, of course, but it sounds true so maybe it is.

"In addition to reducing his revenues and the Pope's revenues, King Richard will lose William's war galleys which are available to protect his men and himself as they travel back and forth to France. As a result, Richard's subjects along the English and Norman coasts will also lose the protection from pirates they now receive as a result of William's reputation as a pirate-taker.

"If William leaves England," I said with resignation and sadness in my voice, "the pirates will no doubt end up with many coins which otherwise would have gone to the King."

"Yes," said the nuncio thoughtfully, "and forcing Lord William out of Cornwall will also distress the Templars who have given him captured weapons in exchange for carrying Templars to and from England and France. It will also greatly distress the Pope whose new order of seagoing priests will be greatly weakened and receive fewer tithes to send to the Pope. Yes, indeed, many distressing things will happen if Lord William decides to abandon his apprentice-training and ship-building lands in Cornwall."

The nuncio was obviously distressed at the thought of the Cyprus nuncio getting his hands on those tithes instead of himself. Good. Maybe he really will try to help us.

"It is," I told the nuncio as he nodded his head in sorrowful agreement, "a goddamn, fucking financial disaster for the two of us."

"Do not despair yet, Bishop Thomas," was his optimistic response. "I may be able to do something with this information if I can get to the King or Longchamp."

I shook my head in resignation and handed him the parchment I had prepared for the Pope to sign—and told the nuncio William had set aside fifty bezant gold coins for the expenses of getting the Pope to sign the parchment creating the new religious order.

Under the circumstances, I added with what I hoped was an encouraging smile on my face, I am sure there will be another fifty gold bezants if the King does something so William can continue in Cornwall as the Earl and hold his lands as a freehold. Then I ostentatiously picked up my purse and hurried back to the church to eat and get some sleep on its dirt floor.

The sun had already finished passing overhead and it was already starting to get dark when my guards and I got back to the church. We will leave for London at first light in the morning—I have got to hurry back to Cornwall to tell William we are almost certainly about to have a war on our hands.

It looks like we may need the services of the assassins, after all; if they can even find Derbyshire, that is.

* * * * * *

I had no more than wrapped myself in my cloak and laid myself on the church's dirt floor to sleep, then I heard voices and noise outside. Then there was a pounding on the church door. One of my men stood up and removed the timber bar on the door to see what the commotion was all about—and it was immediately pulled open.

Three men pushed their way in—and in the darkness the first man in promptly stepped on one of my men and tripped and fell on top of some of the others. All around me my men were jumping to their feet and I could hear their curses and the sound of blades coming out of scabbards.

"Whoa. Whoa. Peace. Peace. We are King's men and we have come in peace. Is the Bishop of Cornwall here? The King sent us to fetch him if he is available."

A minute later and I was trying not to stumble as I walked along the dark cart path towards the castle in the moonlight. There was a King's man on either side of me "to guide you, Bishop, only to guide you" and a somewhat hesitant and uncertain Peter and my other men trailing along behind carrying their bows and swords.

Well, if they have come to kill me, this is where they will do it.

A loud challenge rang out from the castle gate as we approached it in the dark. It was promptly answered by the man "guiding" my left arm; apparently, he answered correctly since the gate opened to admit us. Us being the King's men and me; my men were not admitted.

"Do not leave; wait right there," I shouted to Peter and my guards over my shoulder as I entered. Then the King's men and I followed a shadowy figure holding a candle lantern across the bailey and up some steps and into the keep itself.

Our feet seemed to clatter loudly against the stone floor as we moved along a dark corridor and then turned into a small room. Almost instantly, I was confused and totally lost track of where I might be.

"Wait here," I was ordered by the lantern carrier. He left me standing alone as he and my escorts clattered away. It was pitch black and I could not see a thing.

Well, at least they did not shut the door and it is not a dungeon. I must admit I am anxious; well, actually, more than that—I am quite scared, that is what I am.

******

I stood unmoving for what seems like ages. All I could hear around me was the periodic scampering and scurrying sound of mice and rats and, every so often, faint voices talking in the distance. Finally, I heard the murmur of men's voices and the sound of feet coming along the passage way; and then, suddenly, I could see the flickering lights of several candle lamps coming towards me.

A servant in the King's livery holding a lantern led the procession. He entered the room and held his candle lantern high—and behind him came King Richard, the papal nuncio, and the lord chancellor, William Longchamp.

Even in the dim light I knew it was Richard. I had seen him numerous times during the battles for Cyprus and Acre and elsewhere. He, of course, would not know me from Adam. I instantly dropped to my knees in the flickering light even though as a bishop I only needed to bow. *Better safe than sorry; that is for sure.*

"You are Thomas, the Bishop of Cornwall?"

"Yes, Your Majesty. I am the bishop for your subjects in Cornwall."

"The papal nuncio and my chancellor tell me I have made a kingly mistake in naming a cousin of the late Baldwin of Restormel to be the new Earl of Cornwall. Do you agree?"

"Oh no, Your Majesty, it is more a tribute to Your Majesty's decisiveness that you made such a minor and easily reversed decision so promptly, no doubt because Your Majesty wisely spends his time attending to other more, much more important matters."

Do you think I am going to tell our hot tempered King he made a mistake? Do not be a silly fool.

"It is also said that Lord William does not consider me to be his rightful king and refused to help ransom me. What say you to that?"

"Your Majesty, I am Lord William's confessor and I can swear to you in the name of Jesus that he has never even once hinted you are not his rightful king. I can also swear he has never even once refused to help ransom you. Much to the contrary, sire, he fought for you and bled for you at Cyprus and Acre and elsewhere. He holds you in esteem as a great knight and commander."

Well, William never actually refused to help pay the ransom, did he? I am the one who sat on my hands for William whilst he was off to Cyprus.

"Then why is he not on the list of those who contributed to my ransom?"

"I suspect, sire .. . . . No, that is not correct; I am absolutely sure, sire, his name is missing because Lord William was never asked for a contribution.

"Lord William not being asked was not surprising, Your Majesty. Cornwall has no revenues because its people are mostly poor fishermen and the lands of its few manors are so poor even the Romans ignored Cornwall and never so much as built one road to it. Cornwall's only revenues, Your Majesty, are those from the tin mines—and they all go directly to you as their rightful owner. Moreover, sire, I know for an absolute fact Earl William ordered the mine overseers to increase their production and send you more revenues."

And after a pause I added somewhat softly and in a most respectful voice, "Lord William did all those things for you without even being asked, Your Majesty. He is truly one of your most faithful servants."

Except, of course, he does not like you or trust you or want to pay your taxes or see you on the throne.

The King just stood with his head cocked to one side and listened as I went on to tell him various other blathers about William being such a good man and a loyal servant of the Crown.

When I finished, the King just stood there in the flickering candle light for more than a minute. Then he abruptly turned and walked out of the room with the others falling in to walk behind him. So there I was standing in the darkness as the candle light and muffled voices and clattering shoes of his departure receded into the distance.

"Wait here," the papal nuncio commanded before he hurried off to follow them. *Do I have a choice?*

An hour or so later, the nuncio returned with a servant holding a candle lantern. He was smiling.

"The King has accepted his chancellor's advice and decided to do nothing to replace Lord William; he will let it be a test of arms with God deciding who is the rightful Earl. And I need another fifty gold bezants for Longchamp for providing Lord William with a fighting chance to hold his lands."

Whilst I was counting the bezants into his hand, the nuncio asked the crucial question.

"Do you think William can win?"

Chapter Three

The earl from Derbyshire.

Thomas returned from Richard's court this afternoon and his tidings were not good. It seems Isabel or someone in her family prevailed upon King Richard to sell a Derbyshire lord named Harold Cornell the same earldom we had bought from Prince John. The King apparently did so because Cornell claimed to be a cousin of Isabel's late husband, the late and unlamented Baldwin. What we do not know is if Cornell and Isabel are related or if Isabel is betrothed to him or if she is involved at all.

The good news was Cornell lives in Derbyshire so it would most likely take a long time for him to get himself and his men to Cornwall. The bad news was that we do not know anything about him—how many men he will bring and who among his friends and relatives will help him, how they will fight, and the nature of their experience and ability.

Worse, and perhaps most important of all, we do not have any idea as to who will fight with him and why, or for that matter when and where. Both Baldwin of Restormel and FitzCount of Launceston were aided by knights from nearby Devon. We killed a lot of the stupid bastards at Bossiney and Launceston, but certainly not all of them.

What is worrisome is Cornell knowing something of what happened at Bossiney and Launceston and still being so sure he can defeat our archers. He must be sure; otherwise, he would not have bought the Cornwall earldom knowing I had also claimed it and was in possession of its three keeps.

There were many unanswered questions. The biggest, of course, was whether we would be up against only the Derbyshire lord's men and the survivors of the Devon gentry who supported Baldwin and FitzCount. Who else will be fighting by his side?

According to the papal nuncio, the King will treat any fighting that occurs as a trial of arms and stay out of it so 'God's will' prevails as to who will be the Earl of Cornwall. Leaving the outcome to God's will is certainly better than having the King send his men to help Cornell root us out— but it is still worrisome because the papal nuncio may have been lying about Richard's neutrality in order to gull us out of more coins.

Trusting the word of a King's courtiers, particularly if they are churchmen, is always a fool's game.

Moreover, even if it is true that the King said he would not interfere and would leave the outcome to God, Richard is not exactly famous for keeping his promises.

Just ask the thousands of men who surrendered to Richard at Acre—which you cannot do because he butchered them to a man despite giving his word he would let them go free.

All we know for sure is there is almost certainly going to be a war between the archers and Lord Cornell—and many of our best fighting men are in Cyprus or the Holy Land. The only thing certain is that it is a damn good thing I kept so many of our archers here instead of sending them out to Yoram and Henry.

Hmm. I wonder if Cornell knows how effective longbows and our new bladed pikes are in the right hands and how best to fight against them? They are so new even those of us who have them do not know how best to fight against them.

******

Thomas and I spent all morning looking at our two parchment maps and talking about our men and their weapons and what we should do. A plan finally began to emerge after much talking and pacing up and down and trying to make sense of our maps.

The damn maps are obviously not very accurate, at least they are not about Cornwall—they have both got Launceston east of the Tamar, for example, and Bossiney on the coast.

Only one thing is for sure; Cornell and his men are going to have to come through Devon and cross the River Tamar to get to Cornwall—and the only cart path running all the way to Cornwall runs through Sarum on the Salisbury plain and crosses the Tamar River ford near Launceston. It is almost certainly the route Cornell and his men will take to come to Cornwall.

Thomas says the Romans built a stoned road as far as Exeter almost a thousand years ago and some of the Roman paving stones are still there. I found that quite amazing. I would have thought they would have been mined for a new building or road by now.

It is not certain, of course, but Lord Cornell will likely come with his men in the early spring when the traditional campaigning and tournament season begins. So Thomas and I have decided to take a couple of risks.

One is to do what we think Cornell will do—hire mercenaries. The other is to further strengthen our forces by quickly sending some of our more experienced men out into Wales and the English counties around London to recruit more archers and likely lads to train. England is temporarily between wars so hopefully there are some useful men sitting around in their villages and alehouses who would prefer to fight for us instead of starving or being robbers or labouring on the land as churls.

Sending out some of our veteran archers out to the villages as recruiters is a big risk because they will be gone and we will be weaker if Cornell hurries here with his army. It worried me immensely and Thomas even more. He agreed about sending out the recruiters, but he wanted to immediately recall everyone we have at Bossiney and most of the men from Launceston—he was adamant about it so I agreed.

Sending some of our men out to recruit also means we need places and men in London and Bristol where we can gather recruits and send them on to Cornwall in our ships. *It is unlikely our recruits will be able to walk safely through Devon even if they are in a group of like-minded lads. All in all, it will be much safer and faster if we gather them in London and bring them in from there on our cogs and galleys.*

Who should we send to do the recruiting, and who should arrange a place in London where the new archers can assemble? It was a good question and a real problem because I have got to stay here to lead the fight in case Cornell arrives sooner than we expect.

After a lot of discussion, we finally decided on a course of action—Thomas himself will take our archer recruiters to London on a fast galley. He will take Peter and some guards and set himself up at a tavern or stables. They will stay in London; the recruiters will spread out through southern England and bring the archers they recruit back to London for Thomas to send on to Cornwall. Evan, an archer sergeant from Wales who seems quite dependable even though he cannot scribe or do sums, will take a smaller number of men to Cardiff and do the same throughout Wales.

Our recruiting parties will be led by a dozen or so of our veteran archers who have already received prize monies. I hate to part with some of our best veterans even temporarily, but they are the ones most likely to know who has potential as a longbow archer and who does not. Even better, they will be able to talk personally about our company and the substantial rewards our new recruits will have a chance to receive if they make their marks to join us.

****** *Thomas*

Fourteen archer recruiters and my ten guardsmen will be travelling to London with me and Peter Sergeant this morning. So will about forty swordsmen to act as the recruiters' guards to help keep them and the coins they are carrying safe from the outlaw bands said to be plaguing the roads these days as a result of Richard's and John's armies being disbanded. *They were disbanded and sent home when Richard returned and John was proclaimed to be his successor in exchange for peacefully surrendering his regency.*

We will be going up the channel to London on one of our newly caulked galleys, the one commanded by Simon. The veteran archers will spread out and begin working as recruiters in the counties around London. An additional six of our veteran archers with three guards apiece will be going to Cardiff under the command of Evan.

Of course, I am sailing on Simon's galley—he was the sergeant captain on my recent trip to London; he knows the Thames and the London wharves and quays.

Because it is so dangerous to travel the roads outside London, each of my archers and those of Evan will be accompanied by two or three men who had not yet qualified as archers. Their training to be archers will have to wait until they return.

Our newly appointed recruiters seem enthusiastic about our plan. And they should be—those who were not already sergeants have been promoted. Yesterday, they spent the entire day being learnt by William and me as to what they are to do and say. Perhaps more important for their success, they have been promised "prize money" for every longbow archer they find who comes to Cornwall with his own bow and makes his mark on our company list. They will also get prize money for every archer apprentice they bring in.

We are hopeful for our recruiters' success, of course, but we expect some to run with the pouches of coins they will be carrying and others to fail for one reason or another; we just do not know who will succeed and who will not.

In any event, our recruiters are more than ready to go and I have got a most painful cramp in my hand from hours spent drafting the parchments they and their companions will carry from fair to fair and from church to church. And, of course, wherever possible, our recruiters will travel with the merchants who move from town to town to attend their fairs.

Many of the fairs have archery contests and those which do not will soon have them if our archer recruiters and their coins have anything to say about it.

Our archer recruiters cannot read or scribe, of course, but the parchments each carries will explain he is recruiting archers and archer apprentices to help protect Holy Land pilgrims and refugees and conducting archery tournaments and awarding prizes in order to find the archers and other men he wants to recruit.

The parchments additionally say the archer sergeant and his men are looking for likely young lads whose families are interested in having them study for the priesthood and see more of the world. This should particularly appeal to the priests and monks they encounter. *Perhaps we can find some additional lads to learn to scribe and sum with George.*

I myself will be temporarily based in London with my guards and Peter Sergeant as my second once again. We will have to quickly find a stable or tavern so the recruiting sergeants will know where to send the men they recruit before they set out to find them. Evan, of course, will have to do the same in Cardiff.

Our very first stop will undoubtedly be at a stable since we intend to hire horses for our recruiters, and Peter and I, and similarly Evan in Cardiff, can always sleep in the horses' stalls until we find something better. Hopefully, the stable where we hire the horses will be able to send a hostler with each of our recruiting parties, someone who can teach them how to ride and care for their horses.

Finally, there is the unanswered question about whether or not we should hire mercenaries or deal with the lords who are willing to sell the services of their knights and men-at-arms. We have more than enough coins at Restormel to pay for their services; but do we really want to hire men who may well stab us in the back if someone else offers them more money? And, if we do employ mercenaries to help us fight Cornell, how and where should we employ them?

What William and I finally ended up deciding is to use our cogs and galleys to bring only archers and apprentice archers to Cornwall—and use any mercenaries we can hire to attack Lord Cornell's castle in Derbyshire.

Cornell might think twice about taking all his men to Cornwall when he hears we are trying to hire mercenaries to attack him in Derbyshire, particularly since we are indeed going to attack him in Derbyshire if we can find some to hire. At least, that is our thinking.

****** *Thomas*

It was a warm and somewhat sunny afternoon in July when our two lightly crewed galleys untied their mooring lines and slowly rowed down the Fowey. My bishop's robes and mitre were packed in a trunk; I was wearing an archer's tunic and William and George and my schoolboys were standing on the bank waving farewell as Simon's galley, the one I am on, slowly drifted down the river with our recruiters and my guards doing a bit of rowing every so often to help steer it.

I feel very sad about leaving the boys but try to keep a big smile on my face. My bishop's robe is packed away because I do not want to foul it when I am seasick, as I always seem to be when I am in the channel.

"Do not forget to do your sums," was the only thing I could think to shout to the boys as we drifted away from the riverbank. Then I gave a final wave and turned away to watch a couple of Simon's sailors begin to lay out the big leather sail so it can be raised quickly if the wind in the channel is favourable when we reach the channel. It would not do at all for the boys to see my eyes watering.

The recruiting galleys will stay in Cardiff and London until Evan and I send them back to Cornwall. Hopefully, they will be loaded with archers and archer apprentices to help with the rowing when they return. Simon's galley, I am rather sure, will be coming back without me if I can find some mercenaries to lead to Derbyshire.

****** *Thomas*

London's port and the waters below it were as crowded as ever with every possible type of sailing vessel you can think of from dinghies and fishing boats to great ocean-going cargo ships. Some of them are huge cogs with two or three masts and decks almost a hundred paces in length with big castles on top of their decks at each end.

Our galley was using its oars carefully as Simon slowly threaded his way through the pack of big sailing ships and fishing boats waiting for the wind and tide. The big cogs may be able to carry more cargo and passengers and are less vulnerable to storms, but we can go up the Thames to London using our oars.

An hour later, we edged up against the same quay we used a couple of weeks ago when I visited Windsor. And the same little man with the sing-song voice and funny hat came to greet us. But this time he was all smiles and welcoming.

"Allo, Simon, welcomz back, yer iz," he shouted as he grabbed the mooring line one of Simon's sailors threw to him. "Enz you too, Yor Reverence."

"Allo, Alfie. Ouz iz you and yer mizzus?"

"Quite gud she iz, Simon, quite gud. Iz youz be at em White Horse anight for zum spiritz?"

The change in our reception by the quay master was so different from last time I could not help but ask Simon about it as I climbed up on the galley rail so he could help boost me up on to the quay.

"Alfie and I decided to be friends after I stood a couple of rounds of drinks for him and his missus at the White Horse over there on the corner. It is got a new kind of clear ale the White Horse's alewife makes from cooking malt and adding some kind of berry squeezings. Burns your throat, it does, but it is got a kick like a horse. Knock you on your arse, it will."

Then Simon smiled a big smile and added, "It is so strong that after two or three bowls I can understand everything Alfie and his missus are saying."

Peter and the rest of our guards and recruiters, almost forty of them in all, were gathered behind me on the deck and ready to follow me up on to the quay. I had spent much of the voyage from Cornwall listening to those who had been here with me a couple of weeks ago tell the others all about London and Windsor.

Some of what I heard our "London veterans" tell them were obviously tall tales, but the men who had never been to London before hung on every word and seemed quite impressed.

******

As soon as Peter and I climbed off the galley, we headed for the stables in the lane behind the quay. That is where I hired horse carts and hostlers to drive them the last time we were here. And that is where I promptly ran into a problem—Bert, the craggy-faced stable master, only had a couple of saddle horses left and I need almost fifty horses and as many as a dozen hostlers.

"Not to worry, Youz Worship; not to worry. If youz got the coins, I will have the horsez for youz and youz lads here in the morning. Amblerz they will be with zmooth gaitz for men who've never ridden before. Hostlerz too. And youz and youz men can zleep all comfy in the stallz; yes, youz can."

It took a while but we finally agreed on a price for the use of each horse and hostler for as long as I need them. But one look at the horse shite piled high in the stalls was enough to convince me to continue sleeping in the little captain's castle on the front of the galley's deck so long as it is moored here—and the men should sleep on the galley with us to guard the coin chest.

"Peter, there is a couple of months of horse shite in every stall so we are going to stay in the captain's castle with Simon until either the galley leaves and we are forced to find another place to sleep or the stalls get mucked out."

We took a room at the White Horse last time but once is enough; too loud and too many fleas and rats and no place to piss or shite except in the street. On the other hand, according to Simon, the White Horse is a real good place for drinking even though the girls smell bad. The alewife's got something new she cooks with berry juice; Simon says it will knock you on your arse if you are not careful.

******

Freddy, the stable master, was as good as his word and, sure enough, the stable and its little bailey were full of horses and hostlers in the morning. I was still counting coins into the hands of the assembled stable masters who brought them when the fun began.

I wish I knew more about horses. Some of these look like they are ready for the stew pot.

Most of our men have never been on a horse before and some of the toughest and bravest of them are downright scared. Others were still severely drunk from being introduced to the White Horse's new drink last night or hung over with terrible headaches.

"Whatever it is the White Horse is selling, you certainly cannot drink it like wine or ale," Peter announced loudly last night as he staggered into the little deck castle last and woke me up by falling down.

Idlers in the lane and from a nearby smithy drifted over to watch as our men tried to climb aboard their horses. The men's total lack of experience certainly showed.

Some of the horses cooperated and stood still as the hostlers tried to help our men climb aboard; others did not cooperate at all—they began moving about as soon the men tried to climb on. They were having trouble even with the smiling and good-natured hostlers trying to hold the horses steady whilst the other hostlers tried to push the archers up and tell them what to do.

My men were not much help to the hostlers trying to assist them. Some of them got mounted and then slid off whilst the others climbed on and did not know what to do except hold on tightly to the reins and their horses' manes. And, would not you know it; one of the men got seasick and barfed all over his horse and himself.

I would have found it a jolly laugh if they were not my men and I was not paying out good silver coins for the horses. But I am damn it.

I coped by doing what the abbot told me to do whenever I got over excited—I breathed through my nose, clutched my cross, and said ten Hail Marys.

It must have worked, for soon thereafter my sergeants began leaving for their appointed destinations via various city gates—with every hostler leading one or two horses and half the men hanging on to their horses' manes and saddles for dear life.

Peter and I stood with the now-silent stable master and watched as our men left. That is when we first realise the amblers with smooth gaits we were promised were not at all what we have been given—most were hackneys with bone-jarring trots.

We looked at each other and shook our heads in despair after we finished waving farewell to our recruiters and shouting out meaningless, last-minute suggestions as they bounced out through the stable's gate and headed off to the countryside.

Freddy and the men who brought the additional horses did not say a word; they turned as one and headed for a nearby tavern. *No doubt to laugh and count their coins; one thing is for sure, I have been gulled out of my coins by the horse traders; we need to recruit some men who know horses. But where and how?*

I shook my head in resignation because I am not sure we will ever see our men again or recruit any archers; Peter shook his, I would think, because it hurt.

Chapter Four

William gets ready.

Thomas has gone to London to visit Longchamp and recruit archers, and it is time for me and my sergeants to get things ready here in Cornwall for the very real possibility of a war. I decided to abandon Bossiney and concentrate our forces here at Restormel. Abandoning Bossiney sounded easy because we now only have about a dozen men there under Sir Percy. But it was not easy, as I learnt when I rode over to Bossiney to let Percy know about the changes and why I was making them.

It was not easy because there was a tremendous amount of siege supplies to be moved—bales of arrows, the weapons and armour we took off of Baldwin's men, millstones, amphoras of olive oil, sacks of corn from the siege stores, and empty sacks and amphorae we can refill. The list went on and on.

When I get back to Restormel, I will have to send more of our horse carts and wains than I expected—and they will probably have to make several trips to fetch everything.

There was also the question of what to do with Sir Percy and the men and women working the castle's fields and livestock.

Sir Percy was easy to deal with. With his wife hovering anxiously nearby, he asked permission to stay on as the castle's governor and the overseer of all the castle's lands. He was willing to do so, he said, even though he would have no men-at-arms and no serfs. I instantly granted his request and assured him his annual coins as a sergeant captain will continue—and told him to immediately open the castle gate and pledge himself to Cornell if he or any of his men show up.

Percy was speechless and his wife broke into tears and hugged me when I told him what I am going to do.

"Percy, I am going to pretend I am a scribe writing for you and send a parchment to Cornell welcoming him to Cornwall and saying I look forward to serving under him. There is no need for you and your wife to suffer if we do not succeed in defending our holdings. Now let's go down to the village and talk to Old Bob."

Percy thanked me profusely as we walked to the village to visit the gnarled old man who seems to be the village leader. The village's slovenly old priest came running when he saw us come down the castle path heading for the old man's hovel. The priest and the old man both listened intently and nodded their heads when I told them all the castle's defenders except Sir Percy will be pulling out and what it means for the village.

"You and Sir Percy and all the people on Bossiney's lands are now free and in all ways released from your past obligations to me and the land. Each man will now either have to leave Bossiney or stay and work their traditional fields as tenants under Sir Percy. We will share everything halves and halves and the villagers who have been working in the castle can choose to stay with Sir Percy or take over a tenant farm or leave. Sir Percy will assign the manor's lands to those who decide to stay on as tenants."

Actually, I had told the villagers the same thing last year, but they did not seem to believe it and they mostly did not change their ways. The only exceptions, according to Sir Percy, were a couple of brothers who promptly signed on to train as archers.

Percy thinks it is the old priest who kept them from changing by telling the villagers it is their lot in life to be serfs and they will burn in hell if they leave the village.

"Percy," I said as we walked back to the castle, "when Thomas gets back please remind me to talk to him about finding a new priest for Bossiney and sending the old one on a pilgrimage."

****** *William*

From Bossiney I headed to Launceston—with a brief two-day stop at Restormel to see how our preparations were progressing and spend a couple of pleasant nights with Helen. She wanted to come with me, of course, and I almost agreed. Then I thought better of it and told her to stay at

Restormel to watch over the gathering and storing of our siege supplies in the dungeon cells and tunnels.

Martin Archer at Launceston was not happy about losing most of his best men and all six of his horses, horse carts, and ploughs. But he understood, at least I think he understood, why it was necessary. *Martin's not always the sharpest sword in the room, is he?*

If Cornell comes, Martin will bar the gate and raise the drawbridge with enough supplies to last a year or more. Martin and his men should be safe so long as he does not do something stupid such as making a sortie or being gulled into opening the gate or forgetting to block the mine tunnels and keep guards on them. In any event, I absolutely forbid Martin and Guy from Ipswich, the archer who is Martin's second, from launching any sorties or opening the gate for any reason except to our own men.

"No exceptions, Martin, you are not to put down the drawbridges and open the gate no matter what you are told or promised. I expect you to hold out for at least a year."

I also made quite a point of taking Martin and Guy to the secret mine tunnel and telling them *once again* how to defend it and use it. Among other things, I told them to permanently move some of the village pigs into the little pilgrims' shrine where the tunnel comes out—and let the pig shite pile up so that no one will go in and find the tunnel entrance. They are also to collapse the tunnel so no one can get through it even if they get past the pig shite.

They can dig out the blockage I told them to put in the tunnel and push the pig shite in the shrine aside if they ever need to use the old mine tunnel to escape.

******

Intense days and comfortable nights followed my return to Restormel from Bossiney and Launceston. The men and wagons and ploughs I required from Bossiney and Launceston were soon at Restormel along with more and more supplies and firewood so that it could withstand a long siege.

Other things were changed as well. No longer were the men practising archery and walking together part of the day and spending the other part working on the two cogs we have under construction or whatever else they were told to do. Now it is all training and weapons preparation with every man assigned a place in our battle formation.

Our forces were constantly getting stronger. Horses and men were coming in from all over Cornwall, and our galleys and cogs were coming in with new recruits. Our intake included a number of archers with longbows and crossbows who arrived from Cardiff and London—and the galleys that brought them have turned around and gone right back to try to find more.

One important arrival came in on a fast galley from Cyprus—Henry. He had heard about the coming war and immediately sailed from Cyprus to join us with almost a hundred veteran archers at the oars and more following. He will be my second in command.

There have also been a number of "walk-ins," including a couple of men who were so starved they were almost dead by the time they arrived. And, of course, the lure of food and coins has brought many of the local men, mostly serfs and farm workers, into our camp to sign on as fetchers and carriers and to work in the smithy helping to make more bladed pikes and arrowheads. Several of the local men who seemed to have strong arms made their marks to be apprentice archers.

It was all hands on deck as the excitement and anxiety about being on the receiving end of a possible attack suddenly seemed to grip everyone.

Thomas was still in London trying to hire mercenaries and recruit archers, but Peter Sergeant and Evan were back and we seemed to be making good progress: sacks of corn and other foodstuffs were pouring into Restormel's siege reserves in response to the generous coins we were offering in payment.

Others of our people were making themselves useful as well—the galley wrights turned their wood-turning talents to the making of pike staffs; and the local women, such as they are, were helping with the fletching of arrows and the increased cooking required for our additional men.

In a nutshell, our capacity to wage war was rapidly increasing. Even Helen was helping tie goose feathers on arrows under the watchful and all too admiring eye of old Issac, our head fletcher.

I do not trust that old man; he would hump a frog if it stopped jumping.

******

Rain or shine, every day starts right after dawn with two or three hours of battle practise for everyone— including even the newest of our recruits and all the helpers and fetchers. My personal fetcher and helper, Peter Sergeant, and I are usually there waiting for them when they begin to assemble.

Peter did quite well in London according to the parchment message I received from Thomas and he is now one of our senior sergeants and my principal assistant. Roger, the coal miner from Yorkshire who made his mark on our list as Roger Miner, replaced Peter in London as Thomas's second.

I asked Peter about Roger. He thinks Roger was a good choice because he is very reliable. Roger is also very religious and determined to go to paradise when he dies. He told Peter he was fine with mining his lord's coal until he was told to dig in tunnels under the ground where the devil and witches might live. That is when he went for an archer.

******

Our battle practise conforms to the way Henry, our most senior sergeant, first began training our men to fight on our Cyprus training fields. It starts when a horn blows to call the men into their assigned positions behind a chosen man carrying the flag of one of our three battle companies.

Each of the three companies is commanded by a steady English or Welsh archer trained by Henry in Cyprus and a veteran of either Bossiney or Nicosia or both. Inevitably each of the three senior sergeants shouts and rages as he works to get his men properly positioned.

When they finish, the men in each of the company's eleven-man squads are standing in a straight line from front to back.

Standing in the first three places in each file are the shield- and arrow-carrying pike men from among our steadiest non-archers. The three pike men are followed in the line by four or five archers. The archers, in turn, are followed by three or four fetchers and carriers with extra arrows slung over their shoulders and pulling hand carts piled high with the file's supplies and equipment.

Each file's supplies and equipment includes its tent, water skins, stakes sharpened on both ends, numerous bales of arrows, spades to dig holes to break horses' legs, and sacks of caltrops for the horses and charging men to step on.

Those caltrops are damn dangerous because charging horses and running men aren't looking at the ground to see their sharp points sticking up—until they impale one or more of their hooves or feet whereupon they almost inevitably scream and fall down.

The fourth man in each file line is the file's sergeant and the last archer in the file is his chosen man. And each file stands shoulder to shoulder with the men in the file lines standing on either side of them.

Together the men standing in a file line form a company square with pike men three deep and shoulder to shoulder all along its front. Most of the file sergeants and chosen men, but not all, have been through Henry's pike training on Cyprus and have experience using it in one or more of our battles.

Altogether, we now have just over six hundred battle-ready archers with more dribbling in every day. We also have about three hundred pike men to stand in front of the archers, many of whom are apprentice archers. We also have a gaggle of about thirty crossbowmen in a special company assigned to castle defence at Restormel and about twenty mounted archers with mostly longbows in another special company commanded by Raymond.

I have sent out messengers to all the farms and manors throughout Cornwall. Every horse except pregnant and nursing mares is to be brought to Restormel as soon as the harvest is in. We have now got more than twenty archers who can sit a horse without falling off; it is useful horses we are short.

Our three battle companies are formed up and inspected each morning by Henry and me and all three of the company senior sergeants. Then we watch and comment as the three companies move around and assume various battle positions according to the various commands shouted out by Henry and their master sergeants—such as would be given, for example, if the company is to advance or if an attack by mounted or walking knights comes straight at the company or from the side or rear.

When the companies change position, the men walk in step to the beat of a rowing drum taken from one of our galleys. The required walking together in step is one of the hardest things for the men to learn. Henry long ago came up with something that seems to work—each new recruit has a part of an old bowstring tied around the big toe of his left foot.

So the sergeants walk the men to the beat of the drum shouting "string . . . string . . . string" so all the men's left feet stomp down at the same time until the sergeants call "stop" or "turn right" and such. It works.

Our use of three pike men in each file instead of the two we used in the battle at Nicosia was intended to make it even more difficult for knights on horseback to break through our pike lines to get to the archers. The same for the sharpened stakes which were hammered into the ground wherever the sergeants want them and were then quickly re-sharpened with the men's knives.

The sharpened stakes are something new that Henry wants us to use. He thinks they will raise merry hell on the knights' horses who manage to get through our storm of arrows, leg breaking holes, and caltrops. That is because the horses of charging knights typically wear blinders and are ridden by knights with their helms down. Henry thinks the horses will impale themselves on the stakes just as they do on the pikes—because neither the horses nor their riders can see well enough to avoid them once the knights drop their helmet visors and charge.

If the horses of the semi-blind knights get past the stakes and caltrops and the leg-breaking holes, they will run themselves on to the long pikes with their points aimed by the pike men, with the butts of their pikes placed firmly in hastily dug shallow holes.

The basic plan is for the pikes to be a surprise to the men who are charging them—to only come up at the last minute after the semi-blind knights get past the piles of downed horses and men and through the arrow storm and leg holes and caltrops and the stakes. Only then will our pike men, whose newfangled, ten paces long bladed pikes are much longer than the lances of the charging knights, raise them so they can be seen and aim their steel points and blade hooks to impale the horses and men coming at them.

Some say it is a people called Swiss who invented the pikes with long handles, and God bless them for it, but it is our own Henry and our smiths out in Cyprus who added the bladed hook that can be used to chop down men or hook them and pull or push them off their horses or feet.

In essence, our archers are being trained to fight on land by shooting their armour-piercing arrows straight into any charging horses and men from behind their frontal protection of scattered caltrops and hastily dug holes to break horses' legs and the stakes and pike men kneeling behind their shields. It was not a castle wall, but it was the next best thing when no castles are available.

If we do it right, by launching our arrows straight and holding our pikes steady, none of the knights will get past our stakes and pike men; if we do it wrong, the knights and their horsemen will get past our pike men and in among our archers—and most likely start to slaughter them until they can be pulled down.

And, of course, it is always possible that the knights and their men will advance on foot through our arrow storm with their helms raised so they can see where they are going and not step on our caltrops or into the leg breaking holes we dig. Each of our companies has something special for that too—its own heavy, iron ploughs and plough horses with collars.

Horses are much better than the slower oxen farmers usually use to pull their ploughs because they walk faster and can be made to run when they are pulling carts. *We had to scour Cornwall and offer far too many coins to fetch enough of them. Even some of the manors in Devon began sending us horses and supplies when they heard how much we were paying.*

The job of each company's ploughmen is to quickly and as deeply as possible plough the ground in front of their company so its attackers will have to walk or ride in their heavy armour through both a deeply ploughed field and our arrow storm to reach our pike men.

If Henry is right, the enemy men who live long enough to get to our first line of pike men will be tired and off balance as a result of walking through the ploughed field—and be more easily shot down by our archers, or speared or hooked or chopped to the ground by our long pikes with the hooked blades our smiths added to them.

I think Henry is right; I put on some captured armour and pretended to be a knight attacking on foot. Walking through a ploughed field in even partial armour is exhausting, even with the visor up so you can see where you are going—I was easily overbalanced and pushed to the ground when I reached our pike men. I would have been a killed man for sure.

Hopefully, of course, the attackers would not even get to the pike men because of the steady stream of armour-piercing arrows coming straight at them from our archers' longbows.

At least, that is the plan and it will no doubt work perfectly—until the first arrow flies and everything changes and becomes confused and different.

******

Each morning, after two or three hours of company drill, the men are dismissed for their first meal of the day. From there they go to their individual assignments: archers to practise, fletchers to fletch, and so on and so forth. That is when Henry and I go back to the castle to eat and think. And today we have been thinking about the future of our fetchers and carriers when the fighting starts and particularly about where the best battlegrounds might be for us to fight when Cornell comes.

From what Henry and I could see when we were crusading, and more recently at Nicosia and Bossiney, the lords and knights tend to fight individually because that is the way they were learnt for their tournaments. They charge in a great disorganised mass and begin fighting with whomever they reach. And they expect their men on foot and archers to run in behind them to join the battle and do the same.

The inevitable result is a battlefield which quickly dissolves into a great mass of individual and small group combats between handfuls of men. We hope and expect this will be how Cornell uses his men. But what if Cornell has archers and sends them in first to soften us up, particularly crossbowmen whose rate of fire is very much slower but whose bolts may have a range as great or even greater than those of our longbow arrows?

Our pike men can raise their shields, and our archers can respond by shooting over and around the cover the shields provide. But we have nothing to protect our fetchers and carriers who stand behind our archers—they will have to temporarily pull back whilst the enemy bolts are coming in and then be brought back to support our pike men and archers when Cornell's main assault begins.

As you might imagine, Henry and I and our senior sergeants decided we needed to immediately add practising for such a possibility to our daily training. We should have done so earlier.

Chapter Five

The Mercenaries.

Things are going along right well in London. Winter is almost done and Roger Miner and I have already sent off two galleys and a cog packed with shivering new archers and untrained recruits. And we have got another thirty men ready to go as soon as our next boat arrives; and every man was very much like most of those we have sent already—desperately hungry and thankful for the food and shelter we will provide.

At the moment, our new recruits and my ten guardsmen are sleeping and eating in Simon's galley, the one which is always moored just off the quay with our coin chest on board. It is where our new recruits wait until one of our galleys or cogs returns from Cornwall to fetch them.

Our latest recruits are about evenly divided between untrained men and archers with their own longbows. Whilst they are waiting for one of our galleys or cogs to come in and load them for Cornwall, the recruits live and cook and practise sword fighting on Simon's galley; some of them are so ill-clothed we have to advance coins to them so they can buy hooded skins to wear and sleep in. It is been such a cold and wet winter it is a wonder some of them survived long enough to get to us.

Roger is my new second now that Peter is gone back to Cornwall. Roger's an archer from Yorkshire. Before he went off to the crusades with us, he helped his father dig coal. That is probably how his arms got strong enough to pull a longbow. He replaced Peter when Peter carried an important parchment back to Cornwall with our first batch of newly recruited archers and apprentice archers—the one telling William about the company of mercenaries I may have recruited. *I said 'may have recruited' when I wrote to William about the mercenaries because you never know for sure about mercenaries, do you?*

Apparently, the mercenary captain heard about me being in London from a couple of his men who had talked to one of our archer recruiters. He thought I was recruiting archers for Cyprus and came to London to see if I needed swordsmen as well.

The captain of the mercenaries is a lowland Scot named Leslie. He took a few of our coins and made his mark on an agreement to bring a company of one hundred and fifty men and fight for us anywhere in England. He is to be paid ten gold bezants when he and his company reach whatever English village I specify and ten more each month thereafter for eighteen months for a total of one hundred and eighty gold bezants. We are also to provide food for his men and their women.

It is a very good contract for the mercenary captain if he can actually provide the men and they are actually willing to fight. I am rather sure he does not know what was written on the parchment since he held it upside down when he was pretending to read it before he made his mark and accepted the first ten coins to bind himself and his men to us.

The mercenaries' captain, Robert Leslie, is a big, white-haired, older man. According to him, he and his men are part a clan that lost a big fight over some cattle and land more than thirty years ago and had to flee for their lives. Ever since then, if Leslie is to be believed, they have been moving around and hiring themselves out as mercenaries to fight on the side of one English lord or another.

Presently, they are raising sheep on some of Whitby Abbey's grazing land on the moors northeast of Thirsk in exchange for guarding the Abbey. *Or not looting it more likely.*

As you might imagine, I questioned Leslie rather closely before I parted with some of our coins. Leslie himself is a strange man and there is no denying it—his eyes and face somehow look a bit different.

"Who are your people, and how is it you are mercenaries instead of living in Scotland?" I asked.

"The tale in the clan is that our blood was not pure because my father's father, or maybe his father before him, was a mercenary from somewhere else who came to Scotland and was adopted into the clan when Malcolm was king and hiring mercenaries to fight for him. Always outsiders we was when I was a lad, and so was my father before me.

"My cousin's family was always feuding with us. Pushed us out and took our lands, did not they? Claimed we was not really part of the clan. So here we are—fighting is all we know to do."

******

One of our archers, Joseph from King's Lynn, and three of the guards will ride back with Leslie to visit his men—to see if they are real. If they are real and are willing to move to Coldfield, and then march on to another place, Leslie and I will spit on our hands and shake to accept the agreement we tentatively negotiated for one hundred and fifty men to conduct a castle siege and battles against an English lord for up to eighteen months.

Eight days later the three guards returned with a message from Joseph confirming Leslie's men to be very real and very hungry, and already marching towards Coldfield. So I sent the three guards riding back with a message and a pouch of additional coins for the mercenaries' second payment along with two more of my guards to help guard the coins from robbers—leaving me with only one archer left who knows how to ride.

The message they will carry back to Joseph and the mercenaries is to resume their march and meet me in ten days just south of Wakefield in Yorkshire's Calder Valley. That is about a two days' march from Cornell's Hathersage Castle.

The mercenaries do not know my plan, of course, because they cannot be trusted to keep secrets; all they know is they have been hired to fight an English lord somewhere in England and that they would be paid and fed. They would not be told who they would be fighting and where and when until they need to know. *And I am still was not sure myself about the when and where; only the who and the why.*

Sometime in the next week or two, before the campaigning season begins, I will ride up to Calder Valley with Roger and the rest of my men and take command myself. Only after I get there will I decide whether to attack Cornell on the road to weaken him or wait until he gets close to Cornwall and then attack his fief at Hathersage Castle—so he is motivated to turn around and return.

******

It was a cold and nasty, early spring morning in London. The smoke from the cooking fires and fireplaces was so bad that it was hard to breathe without coughing and choking.

Until a few minutes ago, I had been wrapped up in a horse blanket and snoozing in the stable waiting for a couple of archers from Sheffield who showed up earlier looking to enlist and then disappeared before I could get down to the stable to talk to them. Now I am awake and pacing up and down and beginning to get worried, very worried.

What in the name of God should I do? I have taken a deep breath and said ten Hail Marys, and I am still uncertain.

It all started a few minutes ago when one of my recruiters, Bob Little, who had been visiting villages in Sussex looking for archers and apprentices, galloped in to report an army of mercenaries, several hundred of them, have begun landing at Eastbourne due to bad weather in the channel—and, according to what they have been saying in the local alehouses, will soon be marching overland to rendezvous with Lord Cornell at Sarum on the Salisbury plain. *Apparently, they have been delayed because they were having trouble unloading their horses.*

There are notable names among the mercenaries according to Bob. The big one is their captain. It is a name we know because he accompanied Richard on his crusade— the well-known Belgian mercenary captain and former priest, Albert Kerfluffle. And that is not a surprise since most of the mercenaries Bob saw in the taverns were apparently from the lowlands of Belgium and the Hollands.

According to Bob Little, there is no doubt about it— the mercenaries in the Eastbourne alehouses say they have made their marks to accompany Lord Cornell to Cornwall.

******

We left in a hurry for Sarum—all my remaining guards and, also, all the newly recruited archers and other men waiting for a galley to take them to Cornwall. It was going to be a fast trip; it had to be—I was going to try to use Leslie's men to intercept the Belgian mercenaries before they get to Sarum. The stable master agreed to feed any new recruits who straggle in during my absence and let them sleep in his stalls.

But what do I do when I find Cornell's mercenaries? Can I buy them off with the coins I am bringing with me? And where is Cornell? Is he already marching? My head was spinning.

Everything was organised within a few hours.

Simon offloaded the men I was taking with me and moved his galley away from the quay to make it harder for anyone to rob the coins I was leaving behind. He will come ashore in on his dinghy each day to see if any newly recruited archers have shown up at the stable where the recruiters are sending them and, if they look reliable, provide them with warm clothes if they need them and take them aboard.

For my part, I hired four two-horse wains for the men to ride on and hostlers to drive us to Sarum and care for the horses. I also hired a couple of riding horses for me and a messenger. *This time I had enough sense to require they be amblers or else there would be no payment.*

Our trip to Sarum was bone jarring and fast; helped, perhaps, by the gold bezant I promised our four hostlers could share if they got us to Sarum before Kerfluffle and his men and my willingness to buy replacement horses along the way.

It worked—we got to Sarum before Cornell's mercenaries, even though we had to replace two of the horses and temporarily abandon one of the wains at a village smithy near Winchester when it broke a wheel and we had no more spares. More importantly, by the time we saw the city walls of Sarum, I had an idea and the beginnings of a plan.

******

Sarum was a peaceful town in those days and its gates were not closed or guarded during the day. Our wagons clattered into the city through the Portsmouth gate. As I had hoped, neither Cornell nor Kerfluffle and his men were here yet. At least, there was no sign of them.

I will never hear the end of it from William if Cornell's mercenaries do not come here.

Roger waited with the men whilst I headed straight to the nearest alehouse, the one with the sign of a stag painted above its open door. I could see what looked to be another tavern further down the street. I will go there next.

I jumped down from my horse, slapped my mitre on my head, and entered the tavern waving my cross at the astonished alewife and carrying one of my bags of coins. A couple of bleary-eyed drinkers, a man trying to fix a broken chair in the corner, and a bedraggled whore were the only other people in the place.

"Hello all, and God's blessing on everyone here. Are you the alewife?" I asked the plump, white-haired woman who was almost certainly the alewife. I waved my cross to bless the astonished woman when she nodded and mouthed a silent yes—and at the same time I dropped what was obviously a heavy bag of coins on the table next to her.

She nodded again warily and the man put down his tools and straightened up to look and listen.

"I have come to buy your services and all your ale and other spirits for Saint Epher's Day. Some fine Belgian and Hollander lads, several hundred of them actually, will be arriving in Sarum in a day or two and will want to celebrate Saint Epher's Day when they arrive. That is the day the Church pays and they get to eat and drink all they want in the name of their saint."

I like the name Epher; it is a good name for a Belgian saint, do not you think? That is why I made it up.

"Well, many of them cannot speak proper English, can they? So that is why I am here—to help them by paying for all their food and drink in advance. Just for Saint Epher's Day, you understand. Only that day, mind you, though their lord is rich and will pay for the days that follow.

"Oh, dear me, yes; I almost forgot. Lord Cornell is also on his way to Sarum and will soon be here himself. These men are in his service. He will pay for any food and drink you provide to the men after their Saint Epher's Day feast. Just keep track of how much they drink and do not stop pouring. His Lordship will pay you if those coins are not enough and the Church, of course, will guarantee the payment. Indeed, we will. Such a generous man is Lord Cornell."

With that, I poured a rather large pile of coins out on the table. The woman's eyes widened and her mouth dropped open, and the man came over with the big welcoming smile every alewife's husband wears when a drinker with coins comes through the door. *Good. No flies on this one when coins are available.*

"And how many of Lord Cornell's good Christian men do you think you can provide with food and all the spirits they can drink in one evening until the sun comes up the next morning?"

Thirty minutes later, and a bowl of ale later, and I was down the lane to the next tavern to repeat the process and again lighten my bag of coins. It took me almost two hours to visit all the taverns and alehouses in Sarum and empty two of my coin pouches.

******

My men and I did not stay long in Sarum. We only spent just enough time to make arrangements with all the tavern owners, buy some food for ourselves, and have a quick bowl of ale. Then we went out through the city's southern gate, continued four or five miles south on the cart path towards Portsmouth, and set up a camp off to the side of the cart path in a small stand of trees where we could not be seen by travellers on the path. It was still quite cold, but we have got food and blankets, firewood is plentiful, and we can huddle under the wagons to stay out of the rain.

We kept a close watch on the cart path and the next afternoon there was a shout from one of our lookouts at the edge of the trees. Roger and I ran to them and watched as Kerfluffle and his men began to come into sight in the distance. Some were riding slowly at the head of the column but most were walking. It may have taken them longer than expected to get here because of the difficulties they were reported to have had unloading their horses in Eastbourne.

I quickly put on my bishop's robe, grabbed up my cross and mitre, and mounted up to ride out to the path to meet them. One of my archers, Alan the smith from Tamworth and the only one left of my guards who knew how to ride, mounted the other riding horse to ride out with me. Alan was armed with a sword and carrying another sack of coins.

Roger and the four wagons and the rest of my forty or so men stayed hidden. The men's bows and quivers and swords were under the sleeping robes so they would appear to be unarmed if anyone came upon them unexpectedly whilst I was gone.

This morning I had gathered my men together and stood on a wagon whilst I explained my plan to them and answered their questions. I am not sure they all understood it, but some of them did and they will learn the others. Those who understood smiled a lot as I told them my plan. Their smiles reassured the others—and, although they did not know it, I marked them as potential sergeants and chosen men.

******

It did not take Alan and me long to find the Belgian mercenary captain. He was riding at the head of the column and just about the first person we reached. He was a huge man with a beaked nose that did not look right. It must have been broken and badly set at some time. I rode right up to him, announced myself in French as I dismounted by the side of the path.

"Greetings, Captain Kerfluffle, and a grand welcome to you and your fine company of men from Lord Cornell. I am Robert, the Auxiliary Bishop of Derby, and I am here to welcome you to Sarum. It is upon me to count your men and pay their bonus on behalf of His Lordship. He would like you to camp right here and wait for his arrival."

We exchanged the customary pleasantries, and I found his French to be as strange as his clothes. He had words and an accent I could barely understand. So I spoke slowly and loudly so he and the men who gathered around us could understand what I was saying.

The mercenary captain's eyes lit up as I explained my presence, and so did those of his men. He and his men, I told him, are especially blessed to have arrived here on such a special day. Not only will each man immediately on this very day receive the silver coin he has been promised as a bonus if he reached Sarum before Lord Cornell, he also has the great good fortune of arriving on the feast day of Saint Epher.

Of course, there is neither such a promise nor such a saint; I am just gulling them by telling them things they will be pleased to hear.

"Saint Epher's Day," I explained as more and more of the mercenaries gathered around us to listen, "is the one night of the year when visitors to Sarum get all the food they can eat and all spirits they can drink for free, and women too—just as Saint Epher and the weary pilgrims did those many years ago."

They obviously do not understand so I laid it out for them, at least, for those who could speak French.

"Years ago, the men of Sarum started a tradition of spending one entire night each year praying on one of those distant hills over there whilst all of their wives and children spend the entire night in the church praying. It is the only night of the year when the husbands are gone and the Church forgives women who stray—and they all do and they all deny it and are forgiven. It is a city tradition.

"The women who do not want a man spend the night at the church and leave their doors unlocked so anyone can enter and see that they are good women and they have gone to the church; the others lock their doors as a signal that they are inside and want a man—and especially a man strong enough to break in and take them."

Such ox shite; but if it is good enough story for Rome, it is good enough for me.

******

I could see from his eyes that Kerfluffle was not at all sure of my story and the mean-looking, skinny man who seemed to be his second was downright suspicious as he dismounted to stand next to Kerfluffle. Their men's eyes, however, become alert and enthusiastic when I explain about the women and the locked doors and the need for me to quickly pay them their bonus coins because the city gates close at sundown. After all, once the city gates are shut, they will only open tonight to let the men of the city out so they can gather at the distant hill and pray."

Then I came up with a splendid idea for the captain and his fine fellows so they would not miss the free drinks and the women.

"I have got to count you and pay you, and you have got to get inside the city before the city gates close at sundown. So I will stand here on the cart path and hand out your coins as each man heads off to the city. And, oh by the way, no weapons or horses are allowed inside the city walls tonight because Saint Epher and the pilgrims did not have any. You will have to leave them here at your camp. It is a city rule. Smart, you know; men get rowdy with all the free drinking and women."

The sight of me standing in the cart path handing out silver coin after silver coin to the men as they hurried off to the city was a huge success. It soon convinced even the suspicious second in command of my good intentions and his good fortune. He grabbed a coin out of my hand and hurried off on foot with everyone else.

Within minutes, only a single guard morosely bemoaning his ill fortune, three or four of the mercenaries' whores, and a man so down with a pox that he could not walk, were the only people left among the pile of weapons and the six horses left in the quickly established camp. I waited until the last man was hurrying up the cart path and out of sight before I sent Alan galloping back to fetch Roger and our waiting men and wains.

The guard was tending to the poxed man when I walked up to him with an inquiring smile and stabbed him in the eye with the dagger that is always strapped to my wrist and hidden beneath my robe. It was a good death; he did not even have time to become suspicious or afraid.

The four wains arrived a few minutes later and we start filling them with the mercenaries' weapons. Everyone worked with a real sense of urgency. Even the slowest of our new men instinctively knew it was time to move quickly.

My hope is that we will be well away before the mercenaries can obtain enough new weapons and horses to find us and take us down.

Whilst my guards and the new men were hurriedly loading the wagons and collecting the horses, I waved my cross to bless the poxed man whilst I loudly shouted that we need to hurry to Portsmouth and dropped a couple of copper coins into his hand. Then I gave a couple of coins to each of the whores for their trouble—and shrugged my agreement when they asked if they could come with us.

The women aren't stupid, are they? We have obviously got coins, and Kerfuffle and his men are going to be seriously pissed when they discover they have been gulled and the women did not run to warn them.

Despite our efforts to hurry, it was almost dark by the time we galloped our wains out of the mercenaries' deserted camp; and when we left we did something quite canny, if I do say so myself—instead of heading back down the path towards Portsmouth, as we might be expected to run to put distance between ourselves and our inevitable pursuers, we went up the path towards Sarum and then around the city walls to reach the cart path heading towards London. *I was hoping this would throw our pursuers off the track.*

We moved as fast as possible in the fading daylight, as the sun finished passing overhead and began rolling around the earth to start another day. The only difference was that now archers were driving the wains, and the hostlers from the stable and I were riding some of our new-found horses and leading the rest.

One of our archers shouted with wonderment in his voice a couple of hours after we turned on to the road to London.

"Blimey. Look at that?"

Behind us there was a glow in the sky. It was off to our left rear where Sarum should be; there was a fire in the city, a big fire.

Chapter Six

William Waits.

Summer gave way to autumn and winter without any sign of Cornell or any of his men ever appearing, not even their spies as far as we could tell. It would have been easy to forget about Cornell and his men if it was not for the increasingly dire warnings Thomas kept sending from London.

According to Thomas, Cornell has convinced a number of Derbyshire and Devonshire lords and knights to join him. Thomas says he knows because Cornell is trying to recruit the same mercenary companies Thomas was trying to get to make their marks for us—and he was telling the mercenaries a victory is certain because so many lords and knights will be with them and we have none.

Mercenary companies are expensive even when they are between wars and plentiful at the moment; so where is Cornell getting his coins? That is the question I sent back to Thomas. I was still waiting for an answer; probably because it is been stormy in the channel for the past several weeks.

******

Waiting for the fighting to start was easy despite each day's hard work. We kept a fire going all the time in the great hall, so it was altogether quite cosy. And the men were holding up fairly well. There was always hot bread, and some kind of meat was served six days per week. About half the time it was the chickens, ducks, geese, and old horses the peasants sell us; the other half was deer our hunters brought in and beeves, sheep, and pigs from our own lands. They go well with the bread, turnips, and onions available to everyone on an "all you can eat" basis.

George and the boys, of course, got all that and more. They also got some kind of chicken or duck egg every day, in addition to all the meat and cheese and bread they could eat—Thomas insisted on it. He said one of the Roman scrolls he read in the monastery made much of letting young boys eat all they want.

All the good, hot food and their skin tents and the hovels they build for themselves to sleep in seems to have kept our men healthy over the winter. Only fifty or so died from various poxes including, unfortunately, one of the boys.

The boy's death was very sudden. He suddenly got red spots all over his body and began coughing and shitting in his bed. We try hanging garlic cloves about him to lure away the poison, but it was too late—within a week he was dead, before we even have a chance to send for a barber to bleed him.

George and Helen and some of the other boys also got the red spots and sweats at the same time but were over them by the time little Michael died. As you might imagine, the boys and Helen were quite upset for more than a week, particularly Michael's brother, even though their new teacher and I kept telling them how lucky Michael is because he was certainly with God, since he was such a fine boy.

Thomas was still in London. According to his latest parchment, he was living on Simon's galley and using the stable as the meeting place where men come with information or seeking employment. At Thomas's request, the defrocked priest who was Martin Archer's second at Launceston returned to Restormel to act as the boys' tutor to help learn them their scribing and sums.

The ex-priest's name is Angelo. He is an Italian with a great mop of grey hair on his head and sticking out of his ears. George and the boys seem to like Angelo Priestly, even though he sometimes acts very strange by falling down and going to sleep when everyone else was awake.

Lately, after our morning practises, I have been riding out with Peter and a few of our better archers to find possible battlegrounds where we might be able to inflict initial damages and ambushes on Cornell and his army prior to assuming the best and most defensible position of all, the riverbank on the Cornwall side of the Launceston ford. There were several that looked rather promising.

One of the best was a big open field that ran up over a ridge on the other side of Restormel; another was a long narrow corn field running up over a ridge on the other side of the River Fowey, between Restormel and Bossiney. We could plough it to make it difficult to cross to get at us.

A third site, and perhaps the best of all, was on a ridge covered with pasture land on the Devon side of the River Tamar. The cart path Cornell was almost certain to take after he turned off the London to Exeter road ran right through it. It comes into Cornwall near the River Tamar ford at Launceston. I particularly liked it because it could be easily ploughed and had thick stands of trees on either side where our archers could wait in ambush.

Thoughts of Cornell increasingly crept back into my mind as the weather changed and the spring campaigning season approached. Last night, whilst I was eating with Helen and the boys, I decided to take another look at the possible battlefield across the Tamar in Devon. Accordingly, after this morning's battle practise I led Peter and six of the archers who know how to stay aboard horses down the cart path towards Okehampton Castle and the old Roman road that runs south to Exeter and the Earl of Devon's castle.

When we reached the Tamar, we stripped off our hooded robes to hold them over our heads to keep them dry, and then froze our bollocks off by walking the horses across the cold river. The river was low and we rode across slowly to hold down the splashing. All in all, crossing at the ford was not so bad, just cold because of the rain and the wind.

I wonder if anyone on the Launceston Castle walls saw us cross; since we can see the castle from the ford, I am sure Martin and his men can see us.

We put our clothes back on and proceeded down the cart path into Devon. It was a cold and dismal spring day. We had not seen the sun for almost a week.

The cart path branches off an old Roman road that runs from Exeter all the way to Dorset and on to London; at least, that is what Thomas told me before he left for London. It is the only cart path that runs all the way across Devon west of the London road, so it is by far the most likely route for any army marching on Cornwall. Indeed, for all practical purposes it is the only way to get into Cornwall unless you walk through the fields and trees and swim the river.

******

"Riders coming," Peter shouted out his warning over and over again as he cantered back from where he had been riding as a picket a mile or more ahead of our little body of men. "Looks to be a dozen or more."

"Follow me," I shouted as I turned my horse off the path. "We will move into the tree line and let them pass. Better string your bows just in case. Use heavies if they want to fight—but for God's sake do not launch until I give the word."

Why would a dozen horsemen be coming this way? There is nothing between here and Restormel? Could they be doing what we are doing?

"Do they look like they are wearing armour, Peter?"

"Not sure. But I think maybe some of them could be."

We rode off the path and reached the trees in time to watch the riders come down the path past us. There were about a dozen of them and several of them were wearing helmets and partial armour.

The good news was they were riding regular horses, not the heavier and sturdier warhorses knights typically ride when they expect to be in a battle wearing heavy armour. Good. It would appear they are neither looking for a fight nor expecting one; more likely they are either on a journey to Cornwall for some reason or ranging over the land just as we are—to see what they can see.

Except they did not continue on down the cart path past us. They must have seen us before we moved off the cart path—for they stopped when they saw the hoof marks we left in the mud when we veered off the path and headed towards the trees.

"Oh damn. Here they come."

That is what Peter murmured as the riders turned their horses off the cart path and begin slowly moving towards us by following our tracks in the mud. They were carrying no lances but at least one of them appeared to be carrying a crossbow.

This is a big problem. Our horses are farm horses, mostly fit for pulling a plough or wagon. Whoever these people are they will probably have better horses and be able to run us down in a chase if they want to fight. What will happen if we stay together is another matter entirely— particularly if they have never before faced longbows in the hands of experienced archers.

"Dismount and tether your horses for a fast retreat; stay close together. There are only a dozen of them and they do not appear to have any archers with them. I only saw one crossbow."

As the riders got closer, I could see that two of them appeared to be knights. I could tell because they were riding horses caparisoned with heraldry. The other riders in the party looked to be a combination of older men-at-arms and young squires. They obviously know we are here; they were coming very slowly and cautiously.

"Cover me. Use your heavies and go first for the horses of two who look like knights and the man with the crossbow if there is fighting. Then take the others."

As I gave my orders I dug my heels into the side of my horse and moved out to the very edge of the woods and raised my right hand in greeting. My appearance and behaviour seemed to startle the men coming towards me. They pulled up sharply and their horses pranced around about fifty paces in front of me. The crossbowman had it drawn with a bolt in the slot.

"I am Hugh of Evesham," I shouted the lie as I turned my horse so it was headed back into the trees immediately behind me for a fast escape.

"I am in the service of the Earl of Devon. Who are you and what do you want?"

I shouted my lies loudly as I was clutching my strung bow and a heavy in my left hand—and holding them against the side of my horse in an effort to keep them from being seen. I did not want the men thinking I was hostile.

Not that I am all that good at launching arrows from horseback, of course, but so I will have them ready if I dismount.

"I am Sir Andrew of Farsham," was the rider's shouted answer. "We are toll collectors and we want your toll for the use of the road."

That is nonsense. Farsham is not even in Devon, and a dozen armed men aren't out here merely to collect tolls— and they certainly would not be showing their heraldry unless they were at war or riding in a tournament. They are either a party of outlaws collecting tolls to which they are

not entitled or they are ranging in advance of a larger party.
Who are these men?

It is a question I do not have a chance to ask.
Suddenly Sir Andrew drew his sword and kicked his heels
into his horse's side and the crossbowman raised his bow.

There was no time to even think. I instinctively
kicked my horse in the ribs to get it moving and bent down
over its side to make a smaller target.

My horse lunged forward three or four steps into the
trees when there was a distinct *thud* and my horse began
screaming as it crashed into a tree and threw me off. It was
as if I could see everything happening very slowly, even
when I was flying through the air after my horse went down.

I was sprawled on my side, and Sir Andrew, or
whoever the rider might be, leans forward on his saddle and
closed on me quickly with his sword lifted high over his head
and off to the side for a killing slash.

There was a grim look on the knight's bearded face
and I had gotten my arm up uselessly in an instinctive effort
to ward off the blow. Then there was a blur of arrows. A
couple of the shafts seemed to miss him but the two that
buried themselves deep into the armour shielding Sir
Andrew's chest certainly did not miss; neither did the two
that went deeply into his horse's chest.

I saw the man's mouth open in a scream as he fell off
his horse and I watched as his charging horse kept coming

towards me even as it stumbled and started to go down. It turned slightly sideways and its shoulder smashed into me just as I was trying to stand up. It all happened in an instant.

The next thing I know it was raining and Peter was slapping me in the face to rouse me and trying to lift my head.

"What happened?" I croaked.

"Your head got banged when his horse knocked you into a tree. But you will be good. You lost your horse, though; she is a goner and so is his."

Sir Andrew, or whatever the real name of my attacker might be, was on the ground a few paces away with a glazed look in his eyes and blood still pouring out of his mouth.

"Help me up," I ordered.

Peter and another man, George from Haverhill, I think, pulled me up to my feet and I just as promptly had weak legs and sat down again. The rest of my men were standing around in a little circle looking at me with looks of concern. *Oh God. I cannot stand. Am I hit?*

"Am I hit? Did he get me?"

"No. No. You are just dazed from banging into a tree. You will be fine."

"Where did they go?"

"Some rode off; but not all of them, as you can see," Peter replied as he gestured towards Sir Andrew and a couple of other bodies and a dead horse on the ground in the open area in front of the trees.

About twenty paces away there was a man thrashing about on his side with an arrow sticking out of his belly; just a boy from the looks of him. Further out in the open area I could see a horse and a body on the ground and another horse standing with its head down and shivering. As we watched, the wounded horse sank to its knees and rolled over on to its side with its head extended as far out as it can reach.

"Any of us hurt?"

"Just you, Captain William, just you. And your horse, of course; she is a goner."

Once again, I struggled to my feet with Peter's help. This time I stayed up.

"Peter, do we know who they are?"

"No, sire, we do not."

Sire? That is hard to get used to hearing and would certainly surprise me mum—but I like it. I surely do.

"Well, let's go ask the boy over there before he finishes his dying."

All it took to get an answer was asking his name and offering him some kindness in the form of water to wet his lips. In between his gasps and weeping, we learnt his name was Robert and he was the son of a vicar from some village called Samfield. He was here because he was accompanying a knight holding a manor belonging to a lord who was trying to gain control of Cornwall. They were on the move ahead of the usual campaigning season so the lord's men can get back their lands in time for the spring planting—and the main body of the lord's troops was less than two hours away on the old Roman road from Exeter and on the march towards Cornwall.

The name of the lord the knight and his men are helping is Cornell and the Earl of Devon and some of his knights are riding with him.

******

Robert seemed like a nice lad, so I gave him a soldier's mercy to stop his suffering—I smashed him in the head with a hand axe one of my men took off the dead knight. Then my men quickly stripped Robert and the other dead men of everything we could carry and mounted up to head back to the Tamar. It was wet and windy, and we are obviously too late to find a place to fight in Devon; if we fight, it will be in Cornwall where we know the ground.

It was time to ride hard for Launceston and Restormel to sound the alarm; the birds and foxes will have to do for Robert and the dead knight—we have no time or way to bury them. *And finding what the birds and foxes leave may discourage Cornell's men and slow them down if they stop to bury them.*

Rank has its privileges, so there was no surprise at all when I took a horse off one of the men. I think he was one of Brindisi's Italian archers we recruited in Palma—and left him to ride double behind Edward, an archer from Haverstock.

Peter and I shouted back and forth to work out what we would do as we rode for the river: we will all ride together to the river and on to Launceston for a brief stop to dry off and get something to eat. Then Edward and I will ride on to Restormel to sound the alarm; Peter and the others will fetch fresh horses from Launceston and return to the Tamar to act as pickets and watch the ford and the river.

It was a fine plan and it worked until we reached the Tamar.

It took several hours for our little band to gallop to the banks of the icy river about three miles upstream from the ford. We crossed earlier at the ford and gotten our legs wet. Now we know we are going to get even wetter and colder, swimming our horses across to Cornwall—but we have no choice if we are to reach the warmth and shelter of Launceston Castle without using the ford, which may be being watched. And we know it is going to be brutal because there are gusty winds and sheets of cold rain coming out of the west.

"Well, lads, there is nothing for it except to get even wetter and colder and then gallop on to Launceston as fast as possible to get warm. Let's go."

And with that we spurred our horses into the Tamar and started across—and discovered horses which aren't particularly strong or well-trained have trouble swimming when they are carrying two riders.

We were almost to the middle of the stream before the river bottom fell away enough so the horses would have to begin swimming. That is when Edward's horse started to panic and went under. I was so busy trying to stay on my own horse I did not even see what happened, but I certainly heard it.

There was a great deal of thrashing about and both Edward and the Italian went under with their horse. Fortunately, Edward had the good sense to slide back over the horse's arse and grab hold of its tail; our poor Italian never came up for air, not even once.

I would not have been able to do what Edward did or even known enough to try. But the ice cold water certainly did wake me up.

Less than an hour later, we clattered over the drawbridge into Launceston, threw the reins of our horses to a couple of stable boys who come running out to greet us, and hurried into the great hall to strip off our clothes and stand naked with our teeth chattering in front of the roaring fire in its fireplace. The stable lads will feed the horses and rub them down whilst we warm ourselves.

Martin rushed in from wherever he had been working and I began to spread the word and give orders even before we finished stripping off our wet and freezing winter robes. Martin and the castle folk rushed to bring us dry clothes, heat bowls of wine with hot fireplace irons, and throw more wood on the fire.

Two hours later, five of us rode out of Launceston wrapped in sleeping skins in a doomed effort to keep our robes dry, and the drawbridge was raised behind us. We were leaving Peter in overall command and preparing to lead some of Martin's archers to the ford and Martin and his two sergeants hard at work preparing the castle for a long siege. A siege that might start at any minute, but probably not for a day or two.

Preparing for a siege is something we have discussed many times, and I went over some of it with Peter and Martin once again. Martin knows what to do to get ready with the time he has left—I hope. *Martin is as steady as they come, but he is not the brightest candle, you know. It is probably a good thing Peter will be based here and can order him about if something is amiss.*

In the time available, Martin and his sergeants will do their best to bring in the local men and livestock and send the rest to a couple of more distant villages. It is a plan Thomas and I worked out long ago, although we never thought it would happen so early in the year. Among other things, Martin and his men are to do is to make sure there are no skiffs or small boats on the Tamar for Cornell and his men to use to cross the river without getting wet. And, of course, the little rope-pulled ferry below the ford will also have to be cut loose with someone on it to make sure it floats all the way down to Portsmouth.

We are going all out to make it difficult for Cornell to get into Cornwall. With a little luck, maybe some of Cornell's men will drown or get a pox from the cold water and die.

And also, of course, starting immediately, no one except Peter and his men ia to enter the castle for any reason no matter what tale they might tell; anyone else who asks to enter is to be treated as a possible enemy and sent walking or riding on to Restormel if they do not want to shelter in one of the village hovels.

"Throw them loaves of bread and send them to Restormel or into the village if anyone shows up and wants in, but do not let anyone else in the castle no matter who they are. And be sure to tell the priest and the villagers to open their doors and be friendly when Cornell's men arrive."

No sense in the villagers suffering if Cornell wins.

******

One of the archers and I rode all night and our arrival at Restormel on exhausted horses created quite a stir the next day. We were wet and chilled to the bone as we once again stripped off our clothes in front of the fire. This time it was Helen and Angelo Priestly and the boys who rushed to bring us dry robes and warm food.

Messengers were soon heading off in every direction to sound the alarm and bring in the livestock to be slaughtered during the siege and other last-minute supplies. I was dead tired but I barely paused before I climbed on a fresh horse and rode down by myself to visit our boats and the men at the sailors' camp on the river.

When I got to the sailors' camp, I was surprised to see preparations for an attack were underway as if Cornell and his men will be arriving any minute. Men are running everywhere and the tents are being struck. I rode through a throng of men clutching their weapons and hurriedly loading the galleys and cogs with the camp's food supplies and their tools and bedding.

"How long before they get here?" Apostos, the head boat wright, inquired anxiously in his thick Cypriot accent— and then looked at me in stunned surprise when I told him it will be at least a couple of days and maybe more.

Apostos threw down the tools he was carrying to be loaded on the galley moored to the floating wharf in disgust, put his hands on his hips, and glared at me in disbelief with his head cocked as if I was somehow responsible for everyone's fears and anxiety. All around us men have stopped whatever they are doing and were intently watching us. They instinctively knew from the way Apostos was standing that things were not quite as desperate as they had imagined.

"All we know is what the rider who galloped through here yelled at us. Scared us half to death, he did."

I leaned down from my horse and gave his shoulder a friendly shake.

"It is just as well, my dear Cypriot friend," I told him with a smile and a laugh as I dismounted.

"Cornell and his men really are coming and soon—so it is quite the right thing to break camp and take the ships down to the harbour."

Then I clapped him on both shoulders and loudly thank him and his men for doing exactly the right thing when they got the warning.

"Better to be safe than sorry, of course; you and your men and the sailors did exactly the right thing."

Five minutes later I was starting to shiver and sweat, and a very worried Apostos was having a horse cart hitched up to carry me back to the castle.

******

My return to Restormel caused chaos and, I have to admit, I sort of enjoyed all the attention. Helen, bless her good heart, took charge. She quickly sent a couple of men running up the stairs to bring down our string bed and another to the store room for some garlic cloves. Within minutes, she had me in front of the fire and under a huge pile of bed skins with garlic cloves spread all about on the floor to catch my fever—and then she took off her tunic and burrowed right in with me to keep me warm.

At first, it did no good. But after a while, my shivering stopped and I took a brief nap—from which I woke up to find I had my dingle halfway in her and she was wiggling to get it all. After a bit, I found myself very hot and sweaty and very thirsty as well.

"The garlic is working, Master. Here, drink this."

It was a bowl of breakfast ale, which is well known to be what a man should drink if he is hot and sweaty.

******

I was still coughing and wheezing, and a bit wobbly, and barely back on my feet, when three days later who should ride up to Restormel but one of the men I had left to watch the Tamar River—and the very bedraggled new Bishop of Devon, Henry Marshal, apparently a distant cousin of a famous knight since he kept mentioning his name as if it would impress us.

The good man promptly announced he has come to see me on an important matter and he was pleased to be here despite his hard journey.

It seems he had come with a small party to the River Tamar crossing point where the ferry used to be and shouted across the water asking for a boat. Upon learning there were no boats available, he had placed himself in the hands of God because of the importance of his message and come across on a horse despite the freezing water.

And then, he said quite indignantly, "I was not even given the courtesy of admittance to the castle and a warm fire; instead, they took me to an abandoned peasant's hovel and left me there to freeze."

In any event, he had come, the good man said, to tell me God himself has spoken to him and wants him to marry Baldwin's widow Isabel to Lord Harold Cornell at Restormel. God, the Bishop reported most earnestly, also told him my men and I must submit to Cornell. It is clear, "God wills your submission," the Bishop assured me, since Cornell is the man King Richard named to be the Earl of Cornwall.

Bishop Henry and I had a second and much longer heart-to-heart talk the next afternoon after he had spent all of last night and most of the day fasting and praying in Restormel's dungeon. It seems that God spoke to him again, as he shivered in his wet clothes, in the dark, and told him it was now alright for me to know Cornell was still in Devon at

Okehampton Castle and had paid him to try to convince me to yield without a fight and depart.

Employing the Bishop was quite smart, even if it was not successful. It is also worrisome; Cornell may be smarter and more dangerous than we first thought.

It also seems, the cold and hungry Bishop unhappily revealed, Cornell has had unexpected reductions in his forces and prospects. Mercenaries he had hired arrived in Devon in an unexpectedly weakened state—just before they joined Cornell, they somehow suffered a loss of some of their number and many of their horses and weapons. Now there seems to be a dispute as to how much they should be paid.

Moreover, just before he left to convey "God's will" to me, a messenger from Derby had brought a message for Cornell reporting an enemy force, "possibly led by you which, of course, is clearly impossible," was seen marching towards Hathersage, his castle in Derbyshire.

One of the Bishop's tasks was obviously to see if I am here or in Derbyshire.

What the Bishop told me ties well with the latest news from Thomas, which arrived yesterday on Simon's galley. Thomas sent a parchment telling me Cornell was on the march and he, Thomas, would be leading a force of mercenaries against Cornell's castle in Derbyshire.

I thought long and hard about letting the good Bishop carry some sort of message back to Cornell . . . but I decided against it; it is better he should continue having his visions and talking to God in Restormel's dungeon than talking to Cornell and having new visions in Devon.

I wonder how long Cornell will wait before he realises he will not be getting any information from the Bishop.

Chapter Seven

Thomas runs for it.

The glow in the sky over Sarum increased as we moved further and further down the cart track running from Sarum towards London. Once the sun finished passing overhead and it became dark, those of us who were riding dismounted and the men got out of the wains. For the rest of the night we led the horses because visibility was so poor.

There was no need for Roger to chivvy the men to go faster. They all understood the danger. So everyone jogged and walked rapidly when there was moonlight and we could see what was ahead of us—and we led the horses and walked slowly during the periodic patches of total darkness when clouds moved in front of the moon.

We never stopped all that long night or during the next day; we kept moving as fast as possible in a desperate effort to put as much distance as we could between ourselves and any pursuers. Distance, we all knew without anyone ever having to say it, was what we needed to save ourselves from the mercenaries' vengeance.

All that night and all the next day we hurried on as if the devil was nipping at our heels, which he may well have been. Our only stops were to allow the hostlers to replace the horse pulling the wains with fresh horses from among those we were leading. Then we whipped up the horses and pressed on.

When one of the horses went lame, it was quickly turned loose and replaced without the other wains even stopping. During the day that followed, I rode in front of the wains wearing my mitre, waving my cross, and ordering other travellers off the road "so His Great Lordship might pass."

All went well until we got past Andover and reached the River Test in the early afternoon.

The hostlers swam the horses across, including the one I was riding. They did so despite the cold without losing a single horse. But there was only one ferry and it was very small; it could only carry one wain and team of horses at a time.

Like most river ferries, this one was attached to long ropes and was hauled back and forth across the river by gangs of men and women standing one both sides of the river. It took over an hour. The only thing good about the delay was the horses got a chance to rest and graze.

I thought about taking the little ferry and sinking it; and because of what happened next, it was obviously something I should have done. But I did not and to this day I do not know why I did not.

We were only a mile or so past the Test when danger finally reached us. And it was not from our rear; it was from our front. Suddenly, we could see a great mass of marching and mounted men in the distance off to our left—it was a huge army with all its baggage and it was coming down what my parchment map showed to be one of the old Roman roads coming out of the north.

I have seen armies on the move before, had not I? This one's got near a thousand men, maybe even that much again if you count all the servants and followers in its baggage train.

I galloped back to the wains and began shouting and pointing.

"Whip up the horses. Whip them up, I say. We have got to get past the crossroads up ahead before that lot yonder gets there. . . . Hurry, whip them. Whip them, damn it, whip them."

Oh my God! It is not even the campaigning season yet. But who else could it be coming in this direction on that road?

******

It had to be Cornell. Who else would be moving down the road in this direction? Maybe he wanted to start early so his men could get back in time to start the spring planting.

Half an hour later, I was sitting quietly on my horse next to a roadside shrine at the crossroads; I was counting men and wains as Cornell and his men came to where the cart paths crossed and travellers had to turn right to go to Sarum on the old Roman road. There were just over a thousand of the bastards, and I counted almost one hundred knights, squires, and mounted men-at-arms. They had almost fifty wains.

We turned our wains around whilst we waited for the first of what was almost certainly Cornell's army to come to the crossroads and turn towards Sarum. I was hoping that by turning our wains around we would appear to be coming from London and on our way to Sarum or the north, not fleeing from Sarum.

As soon as the tail of Cornell's army passed, my men piled back on to the wains and we whipped up the horses— and headed north towards the ox ford over the Thames and Derbyshire on the very same track Cornell used to come south.

Everyone headed north except Roger Miner and one of our hostlers. I did not even take time to write a parchment, just told Roger what to say and told him to hurry. By the time the wains finished turning around, Roger and the hostler were galloping off to London on our two best horses and leading two more in case the first two founder—to tell Simon to row urgently for Cornwall and to warn William as to Cornell's location and strength. He is to also tell William that I will be taking our mercenaries to lay siege to Cornell's Hathersage Castle in Derbyshire. Alan will be my number two until Roger returns.

Roger and the hostler will only stay at the stable for a few hours—just long enough to collect any additional archers and recruits who might have come in since we left and rent the wains they will need to bring them north to meet us in the Calder Valley.

He is doing well, Roger is; he is a senior sergeant for sure if he accomplishes this. Now everything depends on Roger and Simon's galley. All I can do is hope Roger will return with more archers and Simon will reach William with my warning before Cornell arrives. I should have destroyed the ferry over the River Test.

Two rainy days later, about twenty-four hours after my exhausted men and horses crossed the Thames at the ford above London, where the oxen cross on their way to London, we came over a little rise and I finally saw what I was looking for—a place where we can go to ground and hide for a day or two whilst we rest. We are not likely to be seen now—we are finally north of the crossroads where Cornell and his men coming from Hathersage would have joined the great road and begun marching south.

We quickly turned off the north-south road and led our overloaded wains over some pasture land and into a great stand of trees that seemed to stretch to the horizon. It was probably the hunting grounds of some great noble. I never did find out.

******

We rested for an entire day. Then it took four more days to reach Joseph and the mercenaries at their new camp in the Calder Valley.

Hopefully, Joseph and Leslie's mercenaries will be there; I do not know what we will do if they are not.

Getting to the valley required us to ford numerous small streams as we passed through a beautiful green and peaceful countryside—filled with sheep and empty of people. The further north we went the fewer fields and people we saw and the fewer pilgrims and travellers we met coming towards us on the cart path.

My arse got sore after the second day of hard riding, so I tied my horse to one of the wains and rode sitting next to the horse driver from then on. It is easier to stay dry under a sleeping skin when it rains and, besides, if I am riding on a wain I can fall asleep. I jerked awake and switched to riding in the wain when I dozed off to sleep and almost fell off my horse.

We did not stop at any of the villages we passed, even those close to the cart path. Women came to the doors of some of their hovels and watched as we passed by and some of the village children always came running out and tried to talk to us; but we could not understand their words and they could not understand ours.

The countryside became even more quiet and deserted once we turned off the main north-to-south cart road and headed out on an even less utilised path towards the valley. The handful of villages we saw from the track on our third and fourth days of travel were small and isolated. We did not see a single castle or fortified farm house, not even off in the distance.

At first, I thought that perhaps the gentry lived off the path; but we did not see any houses or monasteries even when we are going over a hill and could see much of the surrounding countryside—just a few small and isolated little villages with five or six thatched-roof houses and barns.

All the houses we saw seemed quite small, though perhaps they only seem that way because the countryside is so vast. None of them appeared to have chimneys and many seemed to be deserted. They were in some ways very much like those we have in Cornwall—woven branches and reeds attached to a wooden frame, daubed with mud to cover the openings in the weave, and topped with thatched roofs. A hole in the roof at one end lets the smoke out and the rain and wind in.

One big difference is most of the houses we saw did not have entrance doors the way we have in Cornwall or that I remember from the days I spent growing up in the little Yorkshire village where William and I were born. All they have are small openings in their walls that are large enough for a man to pass through.

Sometimes the openings are covered with hanging sheepskins to keep out the wind and rain. Others do not even have door skins. Perhaps the people living in them only hang their door skins at night when they do not need the light coming in from the doorway in order to see.

I remarked on the difference to Alex, from Dudley, who was driving the two horses pulling my wagon. He told me it is because the people up here mix sheep dung in the mud they stick on the woven branches and reeds to keep out the night airs.

I nodded my head in agreement but I did not believe it; how would he know?

"Alex, where did you hear that?"

******

A strange little man sitting by the side of the path was the first indication we may have found Leslie's mercenaries. He jumped up and stared at us intently. I was in the second wagon so I stood up and shouted, "Over here," and motioned him to me as our little column comes to a halt.

"Bishop? Are you a bishop?" he inquired in a heavy and almost indecipherable brogue, and then he said something I could not understand at all. But I did catch the word "Leslie" so it looks as though we may have found them.

"Yes, that is me," I agreed with a smile and a nod as I pointed to my chest.

The little man broke out in a great huge smile and began pointing and motioning for us to follow him off the track. We did, and an hour or so later we came around a little hill and got our first look at the camp of Leslie's company of mercenaries. It was a scattering of wagons and sheepskin tents and crude woven hovels, and it was filled with women and children—all of whom got very excited when we appeared. Within seconds we were surrounded by excited children.

Joseph and Old Leslie, the captain of the mercenaries, showed up almost immediately and, a few seconds later, so did the skinny man who is Leslie's second. They all had welcoming smiles on their faces and outstretched hands.

"Hello, Captain Leslie; Hello, Joseph. It is good to see you both again."

Within minutes, the women and children have been shooed away and the three of us were surrounded by a number of men. They are of all ages from beardless youth to elderly greybeards—and they were all carefully watching and listening. Even my own men came over to listen.

This would not do at all. I have much to tell Leslie but we need to talk privately.

"Captain, is there a place we can sit and talk privately?"

Leslie nodded, and a few seconds later the four of us were sitting facing each other on some freshly cut logs with Joseph standing alertly near. The skinny man sitting next to Leslie was Angus; he is Leslie's eldest son and apparent heir.

The men in the camp, both the mercenaries and mine, drifted over and stood near us whilst we talked. Leslie must have said something, for his men suddenly moved back a ways so the four of us could talk privately. Mine instinctively moved back with them.

******

"Our enemy, the man I am hiring you and your men to help us fight, under my command," I told Leslie, "is Lord Cornell of Hathersage Castle. It is about a three-day walk from here, maybe longer if your women and children march with us."

I told Leslie and Angus everything I knew about Lord Cornell and why we are enemies and what had happened so far. *Well, almost everything; I did not tell him William is my brother.*

Leslie and his son did not say a word as I spoke, but I could see them change and become highly pleased when they heard me say Cornell has taken himself and his men off to Cornwall. They should be pleased—it probably means a siege instead of a battle, at least until Cornell returns. And the old man laughed uproariously and even his son smiled when I told them about the misadventures of Captain Kerfluffle and his men.

On the other hand, they were both highly unhappy about fighting under the command of a bishop who, so far as they knew, knows nothing about fighting and warfare.

"My dear boy," I leaned over and told Angus when he snorted in disgust at the news, "I had not always been a bishop saying prayers and collecting coins in the name of Christ. And I think it fair to say that I have already killed many more men than you ever have, or ever will for that matter. Indeed, I could kill you right now before you could even stand up."

Angus snorted again in amusement. A split second later his eyes got very wide and his mouth dropped open when he realised I had extended my arm and I was holding a double-edged dagger at his throat. There was a collective gasp from the men standing around us, which dissipated into nervous laughter when I smiled benignly at Angus and tucked it back in my sleeve.

******

Almost immediately we held a parade to count Leslie's men and pay the next of the fees required under the contract. One hundred and forty-four men presented themselves and their arms. Mostly, they were swordsmen with shields. Only three were archers and all they had were their own short bows and a couple of quivers of arrows.

With the three Scots, we had a total of twenty-two archers including my guards and the new recruits who came from London in the wagons. There were also about a dozen men of uncertain value who signed on to be archer trainees and come with us from London. We had more than enough arrows for our longbows since we took so many off Simon's galley and carried them here in the wagons.

Leslie then did something quite good—he invited me to speak to his men and explain why we are employing them.

All the men, including our own, gathered around and listened carefully when I climbed up on one of the wagons and told them who we are and what we are going to do together and why. Their women crowded in to listen with them.

Relief at learning it will almost certainly be a siege instead of an immediate pitched battle was apparent on every man and woman's face—and the Scots all laughed with great pleasure when they heard about the way we gulled Cornell's mercenaries and saw our men proudly nodding their agreement to my tale.

Hmm. There were a couple of short bows among the weapons we picked up. I wonder if any of our trainees or Leslie's men know how to use them.

"Captain Leslie," I asked as I climbed down from the wagon, "do you suppose any of your men would like to accept weapons for part of their pay?"

Chapter Eight

William.

Peter finally galloped in on an exhausted horse with news of Cornell almost a week later—yesterday he saw Cornell's men beginning to arrive on the far bank of the Tamar. He appears to have a force of about two thousand fighting men and a huge train of servants, helpers, and commissaries. We have about nine hundred and fifty archers and pike men, plus about four hundred fetchers and carriers.

Within the hour of Peter's arrival, he was wolfing down food in front of the fire in the great hall, I was off to join our army in the field, and Restormel's drawbridge was up and its gate barred. Now we will wait and drill and prepare the field until it is time to fight. Peter will stay for a few hours to rest and then head back to the pickets. According to Peter, the Tamar is still flooding. No one will be able to cross for three or four days.

******

Cornell was coming with such a huge army that we had no choice but to agree to terms. That was the sad reality of the news the Archdeacon of Cornwall brought us in his quest for peace. He was accompanied by a man Peter had sent from his picket to accompany him.

It seems that the archdeacon was so anxious for peace the good man crossed the River Tamar with a single servant to once again visit Restormel and give us the sad news. But all was not lost—the archdeacon offered his services as a mediator. He also offered to collect and deliver the necessary coins so the Bodmin monks will pray for our souls if no agreement can be reached for our departure.

And, though he never mentioned it, he has probably come to inquire about the missing Bishop of Devon and to spy for Cornell and his cousin, the Earl of Devon. It did not escape me that the archdeacon is based at Exeter Cathedral in Devon and lost the clerical duties associated with his office when Thomas was appointed Bishop of Cornwall.

"Your prayers and those of the monks are always welcome, Archdeacon. But, as you know, we are sworn to send all our coins directly to the Pope." *Of course, I did not mention we are also sworn to only send them when we need to bribe him and his nuncios.*

"And did you know that the new Bishop of Devon is visiting us, Archdeacon? I am sure he would appreciate it if you would spend some time with him, perhaps share a nearby room so you can pray for peace together. He is a bit lonely, I fear, what with everyone so busy with all the preparations that have to be made for the coming battles. We cannot have that, can we?"

An hour later, the Bishop and archdeacon were in their respective dungeon cells and doubtlessly jumping around to stay warm and chatting in the dark about "God's will" and their futures—and I was riding back to our battle camp on the hill west of the castle eating the ox joint Helen brought to me as I was leaving. *It was quite delicious.*

******

A rider from Peter's picket at the Tamar ford near Launceston came in whilst I was holding a candle so a couple of my men could see to guide the archdeacon to his new room below the great hall. The picket rider brought a message from Peter—Cornell's men are gathering on the other side of the Tamar and seem to be getting ready to attempt a crossing even though the river is still high from the recent rains.

If our little company of mounted and wagon-carried archers leaves immediately, we can reach Peter and his picket at our rendezvous point by dawn.

The ploughmen had been hard at work for days, and the ground to the front and sides of our intended battle line is ploughed as deep as the ploughs can go from the front of our battle line to the arrow range of our strongest archers and some paces beyond, in the area where Cornell's men might assemble. Only a narrow path in the middle is unploughed and walkable. Finishing the ploughing is important for it means the plough horses are available to pull wagons.

The high waters on the Tamar means the possibility of inflicting some casualties on Cornell's forces at the river ford on the cart path is too good an opportunity to pass up; so I gave the necessary orders.

Thirty minutes later, we left to the waves and cheers of the men who were not going with us—eighteen archers on horseback and nine horse wagons carrying another sixty archers, food for the men and horses, and bales of arrows. Everyone else will remain here under Henry's command and ready to fight on a field where our positions are prepared and they have practised.

******

It took longer than I expected to reach our picket. The sun was already coming up and starting to pass overhead when Peter stepped out of the bushes along the path and waved a cheery hello. *His calm appearance and behaviour was very encouraging to us all; yes, it was.*

"The river's still quite high and they had not started crossing."

Our very first move was to turn the wagons about in case we needed to make a rapid retreat and give the horses a drink in the little stream running nearby and a goodly portion of corn. Whilst it was being done, Peter led me forward to the concealed position where he and his men sit whilst they watch the ford.

And there they are—a host of men were gathered in a camp in the meadow on the other side of the river. We can see their tents and wagons and sometimes actually hear them and smell their cooking fires.

All day long we dozed and ate and quietly watched—and once we thought we saw Cornell himself among a group of knights who walk down towards the ford where they will cross the river. A few feet closer and I would have attempted a very long shot to try to take him.

Peter and I each notched a "light" we carefully selected for maximum distance and waited hopefully—but Cornell, if that is who it is, turned and walked back to a tent in the middle of the camp.

Later that evening, in the dark, we quietly brought our men to their positions high on the riverbank immediately in front of the ford. We have practised doing this before but this time we are moving up to the ford for real.

"Everybody stays down; nobody moves; nobody says a word; and nobody launches until I give the shout."

Over and over, Peter and I said it quietly as we watched in the moonlight as the men slipped into their positions behind the logs we cut down and pulled into place months ago. From here, we can look down on the river where it widens to reduce the water depth and create a ford—when the river is running normally. It is a fine position. Cornell's men will come across right in front of us when they come and we can reach about a hundred paces beyond the other side of the river with our "longs."

I wonder if Cornell's men or his mercenaries have ever faced longbows or know their range?

It is always scary for men to wait in ambush and not be able to see either their friends or watch the enemy approach. That is why we have got the archers virtually shoulder to shoulder—so every man can see at least five or six other archers and Peter and I can see them all.

It is important no man feels deserted or alone. That is when men panic and run.

What was surprising was that Cornell had not sent someone to range over this side of the river looking for an ambush—*or has he and we did not see him? Uh-oh.*

"Peter, send one of your men back to join the hostlers at the wagons and horses. Tell him to stay there and look for people on this side of the river who might be spying on us. He is to run here and tell us if he sees anyone."

Damn, we should have brought a horn. And I probably should have sent the wagons back to Launceston.

******

Cornell's men gathered along the far riverbank and began coming across the next morning. They started having trouble almost immediately because the river was still high and running fast, even though it was much lower than it was yesterday afternoon. They should have waited. *I wonder why they did not.*

"Peter," I whisper, "why do you think they aren't waiting for the river to go down?"

"I do not know. But they are damn fools if they try it now and that is a fact. We crossed when it was lower and it was difficult then. Remember how we lost the man who was riding double with Edward the shoemaker? This is going to be worse and many of Cornell's men will be on foot. Maybe they just do not realise how difficult it is going to be."

Our position was on a bluff of land overlooking the River Tamar. The Tamar is a very important river because it literally cuts Cornwall off from the rest of England—it starts only a couple of miles from the northern coast but flows southerly all the way across England to Plymouth. Cornell and his men had to cross the Tamar somewhere if they are to get out of Devon and into Cornwall.

Cornell's men were coming on the only road that runs all the way across Devon, the cart path that follows the old Roman road to where the River Tamar widens near Launceston Castle and becomes somewhat fordable when the river is low. It branches off from the old Roman road where it turns south to Exeter on the Devon coast.

Usually, there is a small ferry just below the ford. Ferrymen living in the hovels on either side of the river pull it back and forth across the river to carry wagons and keep travellers' feet dry, at least for those who are willing to pay the ferrymen's small fee.

As you might imagine, the ferry and the ferrymen and their families were not here today—as soon as we heard about Cornell coming to Cornwall with an army we paid the ferrymen to float the ferry almost all the way down the river to the river's mouth.

They would have taken the ferry all the way down if it had not gotten stuck on a sandbar. When the war is finished we will have to help the ferrymen build a new one. We need a ferry here.

Cornell's army came on the cart road across Devon and got as far as the ford. His camp was out in the open area just beyond the river for all to see. It started almost at the water's edge on the Devon side of the river; our position was across from his camp on the Cornwall side of the Tamar overlooking the ford.

We were in position but under cover. We were hiding in an ambush where we could not be seen from the Devon side of the river. From up here on the Cornwall side of the river, we could cover the entire river ford with our longbows and well into Cornell's camp on the other side.

It is probably fair to say that either Cornell and his men do not know we are here or they do not know the range of a longbow; hopefully, they are ignorant of both.

At the moment, the Tamar was muddy and running fast and high as a result of the recent heavy rains. We were about thirty feet away from the edge of the water and about twenty feet above it. When the river goes back down to normal, we will be about a hundred feet from the edge of the water and about thirty feet above it.

All day long, for the past three days, we have hidden—stretched out side by side in a row on the cold, damp weeds and brush—behind the logs and watched the ford. It was damn cold and uncomfortable even though the rain stopped yesterday afternoon. But we cannot get up and move about. If we do, we might be seen by the men across the way.

Actually, all of us do not watch the ford and Cornell's camp on the other side of the River Tamer; only Peter and I watch, and we have done so for the past three days by peering through the branches of a big bush so we are not likely to be seen.

Everyone else in our ambush party took heed of my dire threats and has been keeping their heads down and their mouths shut—and we all spent each of the three days silently shivering in our damp clothes until the sun finally broke through late in the morning of the third day.

By the time darkness fell each day the men and I were wet, cold, thirsty, and hungry. That was when we had everyone, except for a couple of watchmen, move back for the night before the moon came out—if it came out at all, due to the heavy clouds that were constantly passing overhead and periodically sprinkling us with rain.

"All right," I finally whispered to the men on either side of me as the sun finished passing overhead at the end of the third day. "Pass it on. We are pulling back. Everyone is to very quietly crawl to the rear and reassemble at the wagons. Take your bows and quivers with you and all the extra bales of arrows. No talking and do not stand up and walk until you are well into the trees."

******

Peter and the four hostlers were expecting us and were ready. They handed every man a loaf of bread and a piece of cheese from the stores in the wagons. And every man got a good long sip from a wine skin.

That was our meal. And when we finished, we would all huddle together side by side in two of the wagons and huddle together under their cargo rain skins in an unsuccessful effort to stay warm and keep our clothes dry. Peter will lead the hostlers up to the river and keep the watch; there'll be no campfires to warm us again tonight, that is for sure.

Our sleep each night was fitful, complete with muttered curses, loud snores, and periodic farts and coughs. I am not sure I really ever slept but I must have done because once in the night I jerked awake from a dream—which I promptly cannot remember; except that it must have involved Helen since my dingle was hard.

At some point during the third night, the clouds parted long enough for the moon to come out and the light caused me to jerk awake. Daybreak looked to be about an hour or two away. It was time for Peter to come back with his watchers and lead us back to our position overlooking the river ford. He knew it well—he had spent the better part of the last two weeks watching the ford and the wagon track leading up to it.

"All right. Everyone up. Rise and shine, you lot. No talking. Time to piss and shite. Then everyone grab a loaf from the bread wagon and assemble around the wagon pulled by the two greys."

Five minutes later, we followed Peter back to the ford. Daybreak arrived about an hour later. There was no doubt about it—the river was significantly lower. Not back to normal, mind you, but significantly lower. Actually, not all the men came with us this morning. I told two of them to stay with Peter because they had loud and uncontrollable coughs. They might give our ambush away.

No sense taking a chance on them being heard and our ambush ruined.

Chapter Nine

William.

The sun was barely up when Cornell's men begin coming down to the river to look. At one point, there must have been several hundred men just standing around over there by the river talking and gesturing. I had never seen Cornell so I did not know if he was one of them.

"Pass it on," I said to the archers on either side of me.

"Stay down and no talking. The river is much lower today so they may try to cross. Do not string your bows yet. I will give you plenty of warning when to string them and take out your arrows. Until then, keep your strings dry under your caps."

******

Something was happening. A rider on horseback was going to try to make a crossing—and here he comes. He made it easily and he was right below us. We could hear lots of enthusiastic shouting back and forth. My men were uneasy—I could see them starting to move about; a couple of them could not help themselves—they were raising their heads to look.

"Down. Everyone stay down and stay quiet," I hissed. "All they have done is sent a horse and rider across. Just one rider. I will hang any man who puts us in danger by showing himself to take a look."

I hope my men know I mean it for I surely will.

The successful rider dismounted at the water's edge, which was now a little over a hundred feet in front of us at its closest point. And here came another rider to try it. This one did not go quite so far upstream before he started across.

Ah, that is why—he is holding on to some kind of line. Of course, he is going to try to bring a rope across for the men to hold on to when they cross on foot.

"Pass it on. Here comes another rider. This one is carrying a line. It is probably for the men on foot to hold to avoid getting swept away."

I spent the next several hours constantly describing what I saw and passing the information on to my men—so they would be less tempted to raise their heads to see for themselves. There was a lot to report.

First a dozen or so riders swam their horses across and two more lines were run from one riverbank to the other for a total of three. On the other side I can see that the line were tied to trees above the waterline; on this side, however, the lines wre being held by the men who rode their horses over because there are no suitable trees or rocks close enough to the water.

For some reason, watching the men hold the end of the lines reminded me of feast days in my old village when we would have tug of war contests between the men and the women and children and moors dance contests between the villages.

Before rest of Cornell's men start coming over, and after a great deal of effort, Cornell's men on this side of the river started what are obviously intended to be warming fires for the men who get wet in the cold water during their crossing. At first they used the wood they got from breaking up the ferrymen's hovels on this side of the river. But even the wood from the hovels was damp—and damp wood and wet flints are hard to work with no matter how much expertise one might have.

Once they got a couple of fires going, however, Cornell's men began building more fires using some of the dead driftwood from a previous, even greater flood which left it high up on our side of the river. When Cornell's men began climbing up towards us to get driftwood for their fires I whispered the order for everyone to start getting ready. That is when we began to string our bows and lay out our arrows—which is not the easiest thing to do when you are flat on the ground in wet grass.

******

Once the fires were going, Cornell's men began crossing in earnest. What they were doing was quite ingenious and worth remembering—each man placed his arms over two of the lines that have been placed across the river and used them to keep from being swept away whilst he pulled himself along with the third.

I wonder where they were learnt to do that?

It took several hours but by early afternoon several hundred wet and shivering men were across the river and huddled around more and more warming fires. The lines across the river were full of men with many hundreds more gathered on the distant bank waiting to cross.

I was surprised they did not establish another rope line crossing; perhaps they have no more ropes.

Once the crossing started in earnest, there were always several dozen men in the freezing water. They held on to the ropes and cautiously picked their way across until they reached the middle of the river where the water was too deep to touch the river bottom. Then they held on desperately and pulled themselves forward, hand over hand, until their feet once again touched bottom on our side of the river.

It did not always go well. Several times walkers somehow got shaken or pulled loose from the ropes and were lost amidst loud shouts and cries from the watchers on both banks. Others of them lost their weapons and their shoes or sandals.

Once a brave soul on horseback spurred his horse into the river in a futile attempt to save someone and was himself lost when he got too far downstream from the ford and could not reach a place to get out of the river.

At least, I think he was lost. I never saw him again after watching him and his horse go under as they were being swept around the big bend almost a mile further on downstream.

Other disasters occur when the shields and weapons the walking men tie around their waists and necks come loose and sank or floated away. The shields in particular seem to be giving them a lot of trouble. The water seemed to catch them and pull the men off the ropes. It was quite fascinating to watch.

Throughout it all a large group of dismounted horsemen stood on the riverbank and watched as the men crossed. There was lots of arm waving and periodic orders shouted so loud we could hear them on this side of the river.

If the men standing near the horses are Cornell and his knights and lords, as I suspect they are, I would bet they are worrying about how they are going to ride their horses across wearing their armour or how they might somehow get their armour across if they do not wear it.

And I still do not understand why Cornell does not wait for the river to be fordable. Surely, someone in his camp must know that men on foot and wagons can get across when the water is low. Or did they think that since there used to be a ferry that the ford would never be low enough for men to walk across? And what are they going to do with their tents and wagons and armour?

******

Finally, we are about to be discovered and there is absolutely nothing we can do to stop it. One of Cornell's men gathering driftwood for the warming fires was climbing up towards us to get more wood. He was dressed like a farm worker or serf, which is probably what he is on some lord's manor.

Suddenly, he realised he was looking at a row of archers stretched out side by side on the ground behind the fallen trees. He stood there gaping at us with an absolutely astonished look on his face for just an instant—and then he got so excited as he turned and shouted a warning that he began tumbling down the side of the riverbank towards the men holding the crossing lines and drying themselves around the fires below us.

I had already passed the word to the archers about someone coming up to get more firewood and told them we had probably be seen this time. They long ago knew what to do when they heard my order to push out their arrows, but I passed it down the line of archers once again just in case— they are to stand up and shoot "longs" at the men on the other side of the river. They were to ignore the men on this side of the river—until I ordered otherwise their arrows were to go at the group of men standing around the horses, the ones I thought might be Cornell and his knights even though they do not appear to be wearing armour.

"Remember, do not start on the men on this side," I whispered once again to remind the archers, "until there are no more good shots at the men on the other side."

Then the firewood gatherer saw us and shouted and it was time to act.

"Stand and loose to the other side of the river," I screamed as I climbed to my feet and simultaneously notched and arrow and pushed out my longbow to loose it at one of the men holding the reins of a horse.

"Get the knights standing around the horses. Pick your targets, lads. Pick your targets. Shoot. Shoot.

"Loose," I grunted the word again as I send off my first "long."

The air was quickly filled with arrows and what unfolded in front of us was absolute chaos and confusion.

For the first few seconds, Cornell's men did not fully understand what was happening. Many of them heard the shrill warning shout of the wood gatherer, and those who heard it instinctively looked to see where it was coming from—but our ambush did not really register in their minds and generate a reaction until every archer's second or third shaft was in the air. And by then it was much too late for some of them.

Hardest hit of all was the group of eight or nine men who appeared to be Cornell's knights and sergeants. They and the horses near them staggered and lurched and moved every which way as our concentrated and totally unexpected shower of arrows suddenly descended on them.

With the horsemen and their horses quickly down, our scattering attention turned to the other men massed on the far bank. They were juicy targets because they were somewhat packed together and not wearing armour or carrying shields.

Our veteran archers made the most of their targets whilst they lasted—which was not very long at all because, to a man, all those of Cornell's men on the other side of the river who could still move began to run or stagger away. Escaping from our storm of arrows was the only thing on their minds.

A minute or more passed before we turned our attention and our arrows to the men immediately below us on this side of the river.

"Get the men holding the rope," I shouted unnecessarily with a grunt as I flew an arrow and watched it catch a rope holder in the shoulder. All the other holders had already dropped their ropes and were running either upstream or downstream to escape.

Mainly downstream; they are escaping downstream towards the ferry crossing and Launceston.

Men immediately below us who moments before had been drying off around the fires and shouting encouragement to the men in the river were now running in all directions as they desperately tried to escape our arrows. A few very brave and very foolhardy men even grabbed up the weapons they had carried across and tried to rush up the slope to engage us.

None of the men trying to climb the riverbank to get to us even came close—if it is one thing every veteran archer does instinctively, it is to concentrate the arrows he shoots at anyone charging directly at him with a sword in his hand and murder on his mind.

Interestingly enough, the charging men probably saved some of the others by attracting the attention of multiple archers. I shot at a man clawing his way up the slope and two other arrows appeared in his chest before my shaft, aimed at his middle, hit him lower down in the crotch because he was already being knocked over backwards from the first two.

Other than the knights who received our first arrows, the men who suffered most were those in the water in the process of crossing the river. Those who were just beginning to wade across the river scrambled back the way they have come. Their backs made tempting targets because they were the closest and had the greatest distance to run before they could get far enough away from the river to be out of range. Many of them did not make it.

A similar fate befell those just coming out of the water below us. They were still desperately splashing their way to shore whilst those who still could move were running or staggering their way along the riverbank to get away. And many of the men already on this side of the river, perhaps as many as a hundred, did get away—at least, many did of the men who were smart enough to start running downstream whilst we were still shooting at the men on the other side of the river.

And not all of Cornell's casualties come from our arrows—the loss of the men holding the now useless ropes left the men in the deepest part of the river desperately clinging to their now useless lifelines. They went under quickly. One moment they were there; the next time I looked, they are all gone.

"Grab your arrows and follow me," I shouted to my archers when there were finally no more targets within our range.

Damn. I should have thought about where they might run.

I picked up a quiver with some arrows still in it and began running to my right in pursuit of the men escaping downriver along the riverbank below me. I could hear my men pounding along behind me as I caught up with the first of the escapers running in the shallow water along the edge of the river.

He was a wiry man with wet clothes and a bushy beard. He saw me stop and notch an arrow as he stopped and threw up his hands to surrender. Too late; his hands were just starting to come up as my arrow entered his side and went deep into him. There was a splash and a cry as he staggered under the blow and fell sideways into the water.

"Keep going. Take prisoners if you can."

I screamed my order to the archers who ran past me when I stopped for an instant to launch at a man who was in water up his knees and struggling to get out of the river. He had a look of horror and disbelief on his face when I took him high in his chest.

******

Our pursuit of the men trying to escape by running along the bank on our side of the river went on for some time. At least a dozen, and probably more, fell dead or seriously wounded and twice as many surrendered before we finally turned back.

We ignored the dead and seriously wounded men we passed as we hurried back to our position overlooking the ford. They were not likely to have weapons or anything else of value.

Perhaps God or Cornell will save them; we did not have time. *Everyone else we will take as prisoners. I have a lot of questions to ask them about Cornell's army.*

Everything was surprisingly quiet when got back to our original position above the ford. There were a number of bodies on the riverbank and in the shallow water below us. Some of them were obviously wounded and playing dead; others were quite dead indeed.

A great mass of men was standing on the other side of the river watching us. They must have thought they were far enough away to be out of arrow range; but they were not. They have obviously never faced longbows before.

For a moment I considered ordering my men to shoot at them. But I decided against it—we would only get a few before they would begin backing up to get out of range. Besides, if they do not know how far we can shoot, we may be able to surprise them and cull many more when more of our archers return.

"Rolph, take Giles and some of the men and go down to the river. Accept the surrenders of any who are faking or lightly wounded. Bring them up here to us. But leave those who are seriously wounded for their friends to care for and feed. Kill anyone who tries to run or fight."

But then I had a thought.

"Rolph, when you are down next to the river checking the wounded, I want you and Giles to shoot a couple of arrows towards that lot up there watching us. Use 'longs' and deliberately shoot so your arrows fall at least one hundred paces short of the men standing over there."

Rolph gives me a surprised look when he hears my order; so I explained with a smile and nod.

"I know you and Giles and the others have the strength to reach them from down there. But I do not want them knowing how strong you are. To the contrary, I want you to gull them so they think they are safely out of range.

"If we are lucky, perhaps the next time we meet, when we have all our archers, they will form up too close and we will get a good cull—so shoot a couple of longs so they fall well short; about one hundred paces if you can manage it."

Ah. Rolph understands. I can tell from his knowing smile and nod. Rolph's got a good head, does not he?

An hour later and Peter and I were questioning our prisoners, and some of our men were being given new assignments. My plan was to return to Restormel with our prisoners to gather reinforcements while most of our archers, including all of our riders and their horses, stayed and held the ford for as long as possible with Peter as their sergeant and Giles as his second.

The men who remain with Peter and Giles will watch over the ford and range up and down this side of the river on horseback to report on Cornell's next effort to cross.

Rolph will ride back with me to Restormel after I finish questioning the prisoners and decide what to do with them.

We will take two of the wagons with us and a dozen archers to guard the prisoners. Everyone else will stay here to guard the ford.

******

The prisoners were very much what I expected—a few were farm serfs with little or no training or fighting experience who belonged to Cornell and his knights; a few others were Kerfuffle's mercenaries who were just starting to cross when the fighting commenced; and the rest were churls, free men who had attached themselves to Cornell and his supporters as tenants and servants. All the churls had brought weapons across the river, mostly swords, and several had extensive experience fighting in France.

Only one of our prisoners was a knight. He was quite young and I thought I recognised him despite his bedraggled and muddy appearance; he was the first rider who crossed the river riding his horse. He took an arrow in the leg when he was running down the riverbank and then failed at playing dead.

He was one of Cornell's knights and obviously a brave and ambitious young man seeking recognition—and therefore quite likely to die before his time and potentially dangerous.

"I saw you ride across the river and I am impressed at your skill and courage. Please tell me how you came to be in the service of Lord Cornell?"

My flattery and the offer of a loaf of bread were successful. The man's name was Francis. His long dead father was a knight with the honour of a small manor near Calais. His family placed him as a page in Hathersage Castle sometime before Henry died and Richard took the crown.

Francis only recently won his spurs. His only experience other than a couple of tournaments was in one of Richard's battles against the Capetian dukes in France last year. At the time, he was serving as a squire for one of Cornell's knights. Cornell took them both to France when he went over to join Richard.

This one's very dangerous. If he gives his parole, I will send him to Launceston; if he does not, he will have to help the churchmen with their prayers in Restormel's cells until I can exchange him or Cornell ransoms him. But if I do that, he will know about them and their fate.

Chapter Ten

William.

In a few minutes, some of my men and I are going to set off for Restormel with our prisoners and the wagons. We will walk all night so we can get there before the sun goes down tomorrow.

I could take them all to Launceston Castle, but I would not—I do not want so many prisoners in the castle helping to eat up its siege stores.

Peter and the rest of our men, and certainly all those with horses to ride, will remain behind to patrol the river and watch for Cornell and the invaders. They will base themselves in Launceston Castle and carry all the arrows and supplies they can carry as they range up and down the river on horseback in groups of two or three men.

I am only leaving behind the men with horses to ride. It is too dangerous to leave the others—sooner or later Cornell will get his horsemen across and be able to ride down any of our men who are on foot.

It will be interesting to see how and where Cornell tries to come across and get a foothold on this side of the river now that he knows we have archers but does not know how many.

"How do you think they will come, Peter?"

"They have still got the ropes and the river's going down, so they may try to swim a few men across here or elsewhere; get them into defensive positions to hold the crossing whilst others come over. Our patrols will carry extra arrows and should be able stop them with our longbows if we find them before too many of them get across."

Peter paused for a moment and thought about my question.

"But that is not what I think will happen," he finally told me.

"I think all his mounted men will swim across the river at the same time at some open area where they can see we are not on the other bank. Once they get across and establish themselves, they will use the ropes to bring the over the men on foot. Then they will march on the ford and hold it whilst their wagons come across. It is what they should have done in the beginning."

Peter's right. Of course, he is.

"I think you are right," I told him. "And I think Cornell will do it quickly—both because he has wounded men to rescue at the ford and because he is likely to know we do not have enough horses to leave many archers along the river."

******

Before we left the river, I paraded the prisoners and told them we were honourable men and would not enslave or hurt them if they behaved properly during the trip to Restormel—but if they attempted to escape they would be hunted down as outlaws and hung.

My plan was for the prisoners to walk during daylight hours whilst my men rode in the wagons; then have them ride in the wagons with their feet and hands tied when it was dark, and my men were walking or sleeping around them.

Sir Francis was another matter entirely. I told him my terms in front of the other prisoners—if he will give me his parole as an honourable knight not to take up arms ever again in Cornwall, I will free him without requiring a ransom immediately after the war is over.

Of course, I asked for his parole in front of all the other prisoners; so everyone at his Hathersage Castle home will know he gave his word and he will be disgraced as a knight if he does not keep it.

What I did not do was tell Francis what would happen if he did not give his word –XX he would be dropped into the Restormel cells where he would undoubtedly join the clerics who have disappeared and were not likely to ever be seen again. So, if he does not give his knightly word, he will either have to be sent to permanently disappear in one of the cells in Launceston's dungeon or taken to our ships at the mouth of the River Fowey and chained to a rowing bench until he can pull an oar on our next galley bound for Cyprus and the Holy Land.

My concerns about Francis came to nought. I was relieved when Francis swore his parole in front of the other prisoners. He seemed like a nice young man, so I took him and our other prisoners to our camp near Restormel.

******

Our return trip from the fighting at the river was tiring but uneventful. We reached Restormel three days later in time for me to enjoy a meal with Helen and George and the rest of Thomas's boys. Before I sat down with them, I sent the wagons and what was left of our prisoners on to our main camp about three miles to the west.

None of our prisoners ran during the day when they were walking, probably for fear that our archers would see them run and put an arrow in them. Last night in the dark, however, four of them somehow jumped out of the moving wagons and bolted off into the darkness together.

It really did not matter. They were not likely to be much help to Cornell even if they avoid starving to death long enough to re-join him.

******

My return to Restormel was joyous with great hugs and kisses for everyone, excited reports from George and the boys about their studies and catching fish in the river, and Helen rushing to bring me warm clothes and a bowl of ale.

We all ate a delicious hot soup of onion and cheese in a hollowed out bread loaf and listened patiently as George and the excited boys told us about their studies. I listened with an approving smile on my face whilst they chanted their sums together in unison, chattered with each other and me in Latin, and showed me the words they were being learnt to scribe on their slates.

Helen just sat with us at the table in front of the fireplace and listened until Angelo Priestly led the boys up the stairs to bed, and the great hall finally went quiet.

Helen and I sat alone in front of the great fire without speaking until the talking in the sleeping room above us became quieter and tailed away to silence. Then she came around the table to where I was sitting, lifted her gown and straddled me right there in front of the fireplace.

Afterwards she took me by the hand and led me upstairs in the darkness to our little corner and undressed me.

"I will be right back; do not go away," she whispered into my ear.

I could sense her moving away in the darkness and then I heard her going down the stone stairs to the great hall. A few minutes later she came back up the stairs, pulled the sleeping skins off our bed, and had me lie on its leather strings whilst she rubs me all over with a warm wet rag. Afterwards she put all the skins back on the bed and burrowed in with me to give me a wonderful touching all over my body.

We stayed awake half the night touching and enjoying each other—and I slept late the next morning until she gently shook me awake and handed me a wooden spoon and a bowl of warm gruel with some kind of raw egg beaten into it "to keep your strength up."

I was able to eat about half of it before I had to get up to piss.

******

It was at least an hour after the sun comes up before I pulled on my clothes and walked down the narrow staircase to the great hall—and found Henry and a dozen or so of my senior sergeants waiting to talk. Even Harold was up from the sailors' camp. They were obviously anxious for news and wanted someone to tell them what to do.

After we shook hands and joked a bit, the sergeants sat on the benches running along both sides of the table and listened as I stood at the end of the table and brought them up to date. My description of the little battle at the River Tamar ford and the success of our archers fetched their growling approvals.

They were all common men and archers, except for Harold; so, of course, they would approve of our ambush and killing the knights, would not they?

"We do not have any idea who was standing around their horses on the other side but one thing is damn certain—most of them aren't standing now and never will."

We talked of many things and I went out of my way to make sure everyone understood how well Peter and our archers performed. The men in our companies, they all agreed, are trained and ready for Cornell or even the King himself no matter how many men they bring to Cornwall.

What the senior sergeants also asked about, and I could not tell them because I did not know myself, was how Thomas is doing with the mercenary Scots he seems to have hired.

******

There has been no further word from Thomas since Simon's galley arrived more than a week ago—all we know is that he has signed a contract for a company of Scottish mercenaries and was off to meet them and lead them against Cornell's Hathersage Castle—and, most likely, put a siege on it if they were not able to take it immediately.

Our hope was that the news of mercenaries' fighting at Hathersage would discourage or prevent reinforcements from being sent to Cornell here in Cornwall. It is also possible Thomas's move against Hathersage would so worry Cornell that he would return to relieve it. Such a retreat would be good for us in one way but bad in another—it would leave Cornell alive to come at us again when we might have fewer men here to defend Cornwall.

Chapter Eleven

Thomas.

Hathersage Castle came into view late on our third day of marching. It had taken us longer than I would have thought because Leslie's entire clan was marching with all of its men, women, and children. *Hmm. That gives me an idea.*

People in the fields saw us marching along the track that passes through their fields and pastures and so did the handful travellers we met coming the other way on the cart path.

As you might expect, they all gave us a wide berth. But for the most part, no one seemed to be greatly excited by our presence. The only exception was a knight who came galloping out of his keep to demand a toll—and quickly turned around and galloped back to raise his drawbridge when he saw the men walking around Leslie's horse at the head of the column with crossbows and the Scots' old fashioned swords on their shoulders.

It does not escape me that Leslie has all three of his crossbow men walking with him at the front of the column. The old swords look impressive, but it is the armour-piercing crossbow quarrels that concern knights and the length of their cast that affects castle sieges. Longbows in the hands of a trained archer have almost the same cast and impact whilst pushing out arrows as much as five or ten times more frequently.

"Captain Leslie, have you or the nobles hereabouts ever faced longbow men?" *Have nobles such as Lord Cornell? That is the question I am really asking.*

******

My archers were walking with the Scots and they seemed to be getting on well. I did another count after Roger came back from London with four newly recruited archers and a couple of apprentice archers. The apprentices will need a lot of additional training to strengthen their arms but might be useful to fetch for us and run errands.

At the moment we have a grand total of twenty-eight longbow men and just over a thousand arrows. Leslie has three crossbowmen with fewer than a dozen knight-killing metal quarrels apiece, a couple of bowmen with short bows and about twenty arrows per man, and about twenty pikes without the blade and hook we add to ours—basically, they are just long poles with an iron spearhead on the end.

Leslie and I rode side by side at the head of the column so we could talk. He likes to talk, and I encouraged him.

"How would you and your men stop knights on horseback, if I might ask?"

"Why, Bishop, if it looked as if knights were going to charge us, we would get behind a line of our pikes and use our swords to slaughter them after the pikes knocked them off their horses."

That was what Leslie hopes will happen; but what if the knights get through his single line of pikes without being knocked off their horses?

"And what happens, Captain Leslie, if the knights get through your single line of pikes without being knocked off their horses?"

******

Cornell's Hathersage Castle looked impressive and strong when we saw it from a distance. It looked even more imposing and difficult to defeat when we got closer. It was an altogether awesome castle—and its ramparts were manned and the drawbridge over its moat was raised. They knew we were coming.

Leslie and I sat side by side on our horses looking at Cornell's citadel. Roger and Leslie's son were right behind us. Finally, I shook my head and told him what I think.

"We will never take it by force; either we gull them and they let us in or we lay siege on the castle and starve them out."

"Aye. That is God's truth, Bishop, it surely is. It is a siege for sure."

With that piece of wisdom ringing in my ears, I watched as Leslie began leading his men in a great circle around the castle and assigned positions to them as he did.

Whilst Leslie was making his initial dispositions, I rode into the nearby village where the castle's serfs and churls lived. It was totally deserted.

The fact the village was deserted was encouraging. It most likely meant some or all of the villagers had taken refuge in the castle and would join in defending it.

The villagers being inside the castle was encouraging because it meant there would be more people helping to eat up its stores of food so the siege could end. It was also encouraging because it meant we will be able to use the village hovels to shelter my archers and house Leslie's mercenaries and their families. On the other hand, of course, having more men inside is bad because it means there will be more men to sortie out if they try to break the siege.

What we did not know, and would dearly like to know, is how many people are inside the castle and the size of its food reserves.

******

It had been three weeks of almost constant rain since we began the siege of Hathersage Castle. So far we had found no one to tell us how many defenders were in the castle and the state of its supplies. And there had been no sign of either its surrender or of a relief force on its way to break our siege. I was coming to the conclusion there was not much more I could do, so I was thinking about leaving Roger here with the Scots to continue the siege and returning to Cornwall. I need to be there with George and my students to make sure they are being rightly learnt their scribing and summing.

My thinking changed and I decided to wait a few more days when a messenger rode in from London with a parchment from Cornwall. In his message, William reported pilgrims and merchants are once again moving between Cornwall and Devon—and the travellers coming out of Devon all say Cornell and four of his five household knights and a number of other knights and many men were killed on the River Tamar by an ambush of enemy archers.

William told me in his parchment that he intended to send a force of riders into Devon in an effort to see if the reports are true. If Cornell is really dead and the threat has passed, William intends to send all of our ships except a cog for training and two galleys back to the Holy Land. He will send them with a goodly number of our archers and archer apprentices.

Four days later another messenger arrived from William with another parchment containing more news. Cornell was dead for sure and William wants to lead the archers back to the Holy Land and raid the Moorish ports along the way.

It was time for me to go home to Cornwall.

—End of Book Four—

There are more books in the *Company of Archers* saga.

All of the other books in this great saga of medieval England are available as eBooks, and almost all of them are available in print. Some are also available as audio books. You can find them by going to Amazon or Google and searching for *Martin Archer Stories*.

Additional eBook collections of the novels in the saga are available on Kindle as *The Archers' Story: Part I* contains the entire first six books of the saga. The subsequent books in the saga are available individually and collected in their entirety in *The Archers' Story Part II, Part III, Part VI, and Part V.* And there are more stories after those. A chronological list can be found below.

Please click on the Amazon link to "follow" Martin Archer and be notified when a new story comes out.

And a word from Martin:

"Thank you for reading my stories. I sincerely hope you enjoy reading about Cornwall's *Company of Archers* as much as I enjoy writing about them. If so, would you please consider writing a very brief review on Amazon or Google or Goodreads with as many stars as possible in order to encourage other readers.

"And, if you could please spare a moment, I would also very much appreciate your thoughts about this saga of medieval England and whether you would like it to continue. I can be reached at martinarcherV@gmail.com."

Cheers and thank you once again. /S/ Martin Archer.

Amazon eBooks in Martin Archer's exciting and action-packed *The Company of Archers* saga:

The Archer

The Archers' Castle

The Archers' Return

The Archers' War

Rescuing the Hostages

Kings and Crusaders

The Archers' Gold

The Missing Treasure

Castling the King

The Sea Warriors

The Captain's Men

Gulling the Kings

The Magna Carta Decision

The War of the Kings

The Company's Revenge

The Ransom

The New Commander

The Gold Coins

The Emperor has no Gold

Fatal Mistakes

The Alchemist's Revenge

The Venetian Gambit

Today's Friends

The London Gambit

The Windsor Deception (late 2021)

Amazon eBooks in Martin Archer's exciting and action-packed *Soldier and Marines* saga:

Soldier and Marines

Peace and Conflict

War Breaks Out

Our Next War

Israel's Next War

Collections

The Archer's Stories - books I, II, III, IV, V, VI

The Archer's Stories II - books VII, VIII, IX, X,

The Archer's Stories III – books XI, XII, XIII

The Archer's Stories IV – books XIV, XV, XVI, XVII

The Archer's Stories V – books XVIII, XIX, XX

The Archer's Stories VI – books XXI, XXII, XXIII

Soldiers and Marines Trilogy – books I, II, III

Other eBooks you might enjoy:

Cage's Crew by Martin Archer writing as Raymond Casey and *America's Next War* by Michael Cameron Adams – an adaption of *War Breaks Out* to set it in our immediate future when a war breaks out in Europe over the refugee crisis and the membership of America and Britain in NATO causes them to become involved in the heavy fighting that occurs.

And Martin's Favourites:

Anything written by Jacqueline Lindauer (*Joysanta*, etc) and Antoine de Saint-Euxpery (*The Little Prince*, etc).